D0510883

The Highland Widow

Walter Scott

ET REMOTISSIMA PROPE

Hesperus Classics

Hesperus Classics
Published by Hesperus Press Limited
4 Rickett Street, London sw6 1ru
www.hesperuspress.com

'The Highland Widow' first published in *Chronicles of the Canongate* in 1827

First published by Hesperus Press Limited, 2010

Foreword © Stuart Kelly, 2010

Designed and typeset by Fraser Muggeridge studio
Printed in Jordan by Al-Khayyam Printing Press

isbn: 978-1-84391-180-7

CONTENTS

Many well-read people are content to do without Scott. For Joyce and Woolf he was a dusty, glittery anachronism. For Forster, he was a simplistic dullard and Kurt Vonnegut thought him the epitome of irrelevance. In Scotland, Irvine Welsh and Kevin Williamson denounce Scott as an establishment stooge, who created the 'sanitised tartan kitsch modern tourist industry'. It's a stereotype as unjust as those of which they accuse Scott.

The largest monument to a novelist on the planet is to Scott. His works were the catalyst for a worldwide resurgence in the novel, inspiring Balzac, Fontane, Manzoni, Galdos, Dickens, Fenimore Cooper, Lermontov and Sienkiewicz. Scott's writing is as profuse as he was prolific, and for many readers the sheer extent can be off-putting; which is why 'The Highland Widow' is a good, if curious, place to start.

Chronicles of the Canongate, from which 'The Highland Widow' is excerpted, occupies a singular place among Sir Walter Scott's Waverley Novels. It was the first creative work he wrote after the death of his wife, and the first creative work he wrote after the financial crash of 1826, which left him with personal debts totalling £116,838. It was the first of his fictions that was attributed to 'Sir Walter Scott' as well as his teasing, pseudonymous alter-ego 'The Author of Waverley'. Indeed, the first edition even included the public speech where he avowed the authorship. Between *Woodstock* and *Chronicles of the Canongate* was the longest gap ever between Scott fictions – a whole eighteen months. It was also – importantly – not a novel.

It was originally published on 5th November 1827 in two volumes rather than the usual triple-decker format, for reasons of pure financial expediency – Scott had made contracts with his erstwhile publisher Constable for an unnamed three-volume novel, and keeping *Chronicles of the Canongate* a volume shy of that number also kept it out of the hands of Constable and Scott's creditors. At that time, he was desperately trying to maximise his production: *Chronicles of the Canongate* comes between his seven-volume *Life of Napoleon* and before his children's history of Scotland, *Tales of a Grandfather*. At the same time he was advertising a forthcoming edition of Shakespeare that never materialised, as well as writing occasional pamphlets, reviews and closet dramas and the contracted novels.

Although the second series of *Chronicles of the Canongate* was a full-length novel (usually referred to as *The Fair Maid of Perth, or Saint Valentine's Day*), the first series was a collection of shorter works: 'The Highland Widow', 'The Two Drovers' and 'The Surgeon's Daughter'. These were bound together with a framing narrative, introducing another of Scott's surrogate narrators, like Captain Clutterbuck, Dr Jonas Dryasdust and Jedediah Cleishbotham and Peter Pattieson in *Tales of My Landlord*.

In *Chronicles of the Canongate*, the substitute author is one Chrystal Croftangry, and the descriptions of his situation and reasons for assembling the book are far more fleshed out (seven introductory chapters) than for any of Scott's previous puppets – and Croftangry shares much more with Scott than any of his predecessors. It is as if having acknowledged that he is 'The Great Unknown', Scott can give full flight to his shadow-play of authorship.

Croftangry, as a dissolute young man, had sought the sanctuary of Holyrood Park at the foot of the Canongate, in order to escape his debtors – a plan of action that Scott himself seriously considered when the extent of the crash became evident. Having extricated himself from his legal wrangles, Croftangry went abroad, made a moderate fortune and returned to Edinburgh a reformed character. He is mildly cantankerous and more than slightly rueful, and John Buchan, in his life of Scott, compares the characterisation of Croftangry and his circle as similar to 'the best work of Tourgeniev'.

Scott provides some humorous interludes where Croftangry, casting around for a purpose, revisits his childhood home. The estate was sold to the owner of a cotton mill, and the old castle demolished to make way for a new 'huge, lumping four-square pile of freestone', although it is now 'going to decay, without having been inhabited'. Commercial speculation had bankrupted that family as well, and a melancholy Croftangry quickly realises that reinhabiting the past is an impossibility (especially since the local inn is run by his mother's former servant, who has little except sharp reproaches and a needling conscience for Chrystal).

Instead, he recaptures the past in the form of narratives. 'The object of the whole publication is to throw some light on the manners of Scotland as they were, and to contrast them occasionally with those of the present day', with the caveat that he will 'pledge [him]self to no particular line of subjects'.

There is understated humour in Croftangry's ambitions for his work. Given that Scott was the most famous author in the world at the time, with editions pirated in America and India in his lifetime, reading Croftangry's pseudo-humble assertion that he is 'ambitious that [his] compositions, though having their origin in the Valley of Holyrood... should cross the Forth, astonish the long town of Kirkcaldy, enchant the skippers and colliers of the East of Fife, venture even into the classic arcades of St Andrews' is as knowing as it is charming.

But the humour is marbled with anger: 'As for a southward direction, it is not to be hoped for in my fondest dreams. I am informed that Scottish literature, like Scottish whisky, will be presently laid under a prohibitory duty.' London publishers had raged against the 'Scotch Monopoly' in the early 1820s – now it was London-based creditors who were proving most recalcitrant to make terms with Scott.

Croftangry obtains the story of the Highland Widow from a 'blood relative in the Scottish sense – Heaven knows how many degrees removed – and friend in the sense of Old England', Mrs Bethune Baliol, based on Scott's friend and great-aunt Mrs Murray Keith.

In Lockhart's life of Scott, there is a noteworthy anecdote about Mrs Murray Keith. She once asked Scott if she might borrow a copy of the works of Restoration writer Mrs Aphra Behn. She later returns the volume, saying, 'Take back your bonny Mrs Behn; and, if you will take my advice, put her in the fire, for I found it impossible to get through the very first novel. But is it not a very odd thing that I, an old woman of eighty and upwards, sitting alone, feel myself ashamed to read a book which, sixty years ago, I have heard read aloud for the amusement of large circles, consisting of the first and most creditable society in London?' Mrs Keith learns a lesson about changing taste in the same way as her fictional counterpart will learn a lesson about changing mores, and in each case it is hardly a cause for celebration.

Again, a note of deep melancholy slips into the Croftangry narrative: the story eventually comes with news of Mrs Baliol's demise. Scott always enjoyed constructing elaborate chains between the subject of the story and the storyteller, and 'The Highland Widow' has one of the most convoluted: from the Widow herself, to the Highland postilion that Mrs Baliol hires on her tour of the Highlands when she sees the Widow (Scott has a neat dig at himself when he has Mrs Baliol proclaim her source 'Neither bard nor sennachie… nor monk, nor hermit, the approved authorities for old traditions'), from Mrs Baliol to Croftangry, who in turn gets the approval of the story from his Gaelic-speaking Highland housekeep, Janet MacEvoy. 'It is,' says Scott with typically wry self-deprecation, 'but a very simple tale, and may have no interest for persons beyond Janet's rank of life or understanding.' Janet can later disavow the tale: before 'The Two Drovers' she berates Croftangry, saying, 'I am sure you know a hundred tales better than that about Hamish MacTavish, for it was but about a young cateran and an auld carline, when all's done; and if they had burned the rudas queen for a witch, I am thinking, maybe they would not have tyned [suffered the loss of] their coals.'

So much for the teller. The tale itself received a favourable reception – most critics concentrated on the failings of 'The Surgeon's Daughter', which, to be fair, does end with an elephant stamping on the villain. That Scott had returned, and returned to his native soil, was celebrated. The *Gentleman's Magazine* described Elspat MacTavish, the Widow, as being of a particular type in which Scott excelled – an old woman with the 'tinge of the supernatural elevating the criminal into a region where she is secure from disgust, and where the fear of the beholder is not unmixed with veneration', adding that she was 'the best of the author's creations, not excepting Meg Merrilees [the gypsy in *Guy Mannering*, and a perennial Scott favourite] herself'. The resounding, qualified praise was *'Scott's lees is better than other men's wine!'*

The story is simple: Elspat's husband was, if you permit the anachronism, a gangster who 'esteemed it shame to want anything that could be had for the taking' and extorted 'protection money' from the farmers. After being 'out' in the 1745 Jacobite Rebellion he was outlawed as a traitor and fell by the shoot-to-kill policy of the Hanoverian 'Redcoats'. Elspat's hopes lie with her son, Tavish, whom she expects to continue in his father's career. He, however, has other ideas, and has donned the red coat himself, in order to become a soldier and fight in America for the Hanoverians – ironically, about to be defeated themselves. Elspat and Tavish have lives far from the centres of political power, yet their clash is representative of the remorseless tide of history itself. And for once, Scott's attention is fixed on the wrack and jetsam of that tide.

A simple story, but one that examines a complex psychology of guilt, pride, trauma, obstinacy and pathological nostalgia. The normal Waverley Novel would reconcile difference while commemorating the sincerity of the defeated – whether Saxons and Normans or Jacobites and Hanoverians – but 'The Highland Widow' refuses the progressive assimilation. There is no hybrid child and happy wedding, but proxy infanticide and persisting fury. You can tell why Mrs Baliol only wants the story to come out after her death, why Janet wants a different Highland story, why Croftangry, in his bemused and sly way, wants the story not to be known in Great Britain, only in his own cranny of Scotland. The story says that forgiveness might not be accepted, and grievances still burn decades later.

Scott made the modern Scotland, and made the very Highlands where Mrs Baliol was a tourist (rather than an anthropological explorer), a tourist destination – the SS *Walter Scott* still chunters up Loch Katrine. His novels are never propagandist, or shortbread tin cliché. But only in 'The Highland Widow' did his guilty conscience surreptitiously take up the quill. Edward Waverley is allowed to waver, but Elspat is adamant. Scott couched this tale in reams of prevarication, whispers, blimpish grumbles and buck-shifting, but the story burns through its fake masquerades. Scott cottoned on to a sectarian, intransigent version of Scottishness in particular and identity in general, and shrank away. The story, stripped of its hums and haas and maybes and whatnots, is about to begin. They are the words of a man who has just lost everything.

– Stuart Kelly, 2010

The Highland Widow

CHAPTER I

It wound as near as near could be,
But what it is she cannot tell;
On the other side it seem'd to be,
Of the huge broad-breasted old oak-tree.
                                    – Coleridge.

Mrs Bethune Baliol's memorandum begins thus:–

It is five-and-thirty, or perhaps nearer forty years ago, since, to relieve the dejection of spirits occasioned by a great family loss sustained two or three months before, I undertook what was called the short Highland tour. This had become in some degree fashionable, but though the military roads were excellent, yet the accommodation was so indifferent that it was reckoned a little adventure to accomplish it. Besides, the Highlands, though now as peaceable as any part of King George's dominions, was a sound which still carried terror while so many survived who had witnessed the insurrection of 1745, and a vague idea of fear was impressed on many as they looked from the towers of Stirling northward to the huge chain of mountains, which rises like a dusky rampart to conceal in its recesses a people whose dress, manners and language differed still very much from those of their Lowland countrymen. For my part, I come of a race not greatly subject to apprehensions arising from imagination only. I had some Highland relatives, knew several of their families of distinction, and, though only having the company of my bower-maiden, Mrs Alice Lambskin, I went on my journey fearless.

But then I had a guide and cicerone almost equal to Greatheart in the *Pilgrim's Progress*, in no less a person than

Donald MacLeish, the postilion whom I hired at Stirling, with a pair of able-bodied horses as steady as Donald himself, to drag my carriage, my duenna and myself wheresoever it was my pleasure to go.

Donald MacLeish was one of a race of post-boys, whom, I suppose, mailcoaches and steamboats have put out of fashion. They were to be found chiefly at Perth, Stirling, or Glasgow, where they and their horses were usually hired by travellers, or tourists, to accomplish such journeys of business or pleasure as they might have to perform in the land of the Gael. This class of persons approached to the character of what is called abroad a *conducteur*, or might be compared to the sailing master on board a British ship of war, who follows out after his own manner the course which the captain commands him to observe. You explained to your postilion the length of your tour, and the objects you were desirous it should embrace, and you found him perfectly competent to fix the places of rest or refreshment, with due attention that those should be chosen with reference to your convenience, and to any points of interest which you might desire to visit.

The qualifications of such a person were necessarily much superior to those of the 'first ready', who gallops thrice a day over the same ten miles. Donald MacLeish, besides being quite alert at repairing all ordinary accidents to his horses and carriage, and in making shift to support them, where forage was scarce, with such substitutes as bannocks and cakes, was likewise a man of intellectual resources. He had acquired a general knowledge of the traditional stories of the country which he had traversed so often, and, if encouraged (for Donald was a man of the most decorous reserve), he would willingly point out to you the site of the principal clan-battles, and recount the most remarkable legends by which the road,

4

and the objects which occurred in travelling it, had been distinguished. There was some originality in the man's habits of thinking and expressing himself, his turn for legendary lore strangely contrasting with a portion of the knowing shrewdness belonging to his actual occupation, which made his conversation amuse the way well enough.

Add to this, Donald knew all his peculiar duties in the country which he traversed so frequently. He could tell, to a day, when they would 'be killing' lamb at Tyndrum or Glenuilt, so that the stranger would have some chance of being fed like a Christian, and knew to a mile the last village where it was possible to procure a wheaten loaf, for the guidance of those who were little familiar with the Land of Cakes. He was acquainted with the road every mile, and could tell to an inch which side of a Highland bridge was passable, which decidedly dangerous.* In short, Donald MacLeish was not only our faithful attendant and steady servant, but our humble and obliging friend, and though I have known the half-classical cicerone of Italy, the talkative French *valet-de-place*, and even the muleteer of Spain, who piques himself on being a maize-eater, and whose honour is not to be questioned without danger, I do not think I have ever had so sensible and intelligent a guide.

Our motions were of course under Donald's direction, and it frequently happened, when the weather was serene, that we preferred halting to rest his horses even where there was no established stage, and taking our refreshment under a crag, from which leaped a waterfall, or beside the verge of a fountain, enamelled with verdant turf and wildflowers. Donald had an eye for such spots, and though he had, I dare say, never

* This is, or was at least, a necessary accomplishment. In one of the most beautiful districts of the Highlands was, not many years since, a bridge bearing this startling caution, 'Keep to the right side, the left being dangerous.'

read *Gil Blas* or *Don Quixote*, yet he chose such halting-places as Le Sage or Cervantes would have described. Very often, as he observed the pleasure I took in conversing with the country people, he would manage to fix our place of rest near a cottage where there was some old Gael, whose broadsword had blazed at Falkirk or Preston, and who seemed the frail yet faithful record of times which had passed away. Or he would contrive to quarter us, as far as a cup of tea went, upon the hospitality of some parish minister of worth and intelligence, or some country family of the better class, who mingled with the wild simplicity of their original manners, and their ready and hospitable welcome, a sort of courtesy belonging to a people, the lowest of whom are accustomed to consider themselves as being, according to the Spanish phrase, 'as good gentlemen as the king, only not quite so rich.'

To all such persons Donald MacLeish was well known, and his introduction passed as current as if we had brought letters from some high chief of the country.

Sometimes it happened that the Highland hospitality which welcomed us with all the variety of mountain fare, preparations of milk and eggs, and girdle-cakes of various kinds, as well as more substantial dainties, according to the inhabitant's means of regaling the passenger, descended rather too exuberantly on Donald MacLeish in the shape of mountain dew. Poor Donald! he was on such occasions like Gideon's fleece, moist with the noble element, which, of course, fell not on us. But it was his only fault, and when pressed to drink *doch-an-dorroch* to my ladyship's good health, it would have been ill taken to have refused the pledge, nor was he willing to do such discourtesy. It was, I repeat, his only fault, nor had we any great right to complain, for if it rendered him a little more talkative, it augmented his ordinary share of punctilious civility, and he only drove slower, and talked longer and more pompously than when he had not come by a drop of usquebaugh. It was, we remarked, only on such occasions that Donald talked with an air of importance of the family of MacLeish, and we had no title to be scrupulous in censuring a foible the consequences of which were confined within such innocent limits.

We became so much accustomed to Donald's mode of managing us, that we observed with some interest the art which he used to produce a little agreeable surprise, by concealing from us the spot where he proposed our halt to be made, when it was of an unusual and interesting character. This was so much his wont, that when he made apologies at setting off, for being obliged to stop in some strange solitary place, till the horses should eat the corn which he brought on with them for that purpose, our imagination used to be on the stretch to guess what romantic retreat he had secretly fixed upon for our noontide baiting place.

We had spent the greater part of the morning at the delightful village of Dalmally, and had gone upon the lake under the guidance of the excellent clergyman who was then incumbent at Glenorquhy,* and had heard a hundred legends of the stern chiefs of Loch Awe, Duncan with the thrum bonnet, and the other lords of the now mouldering towers of Kilchurn. Thus it was later than usual when we set out on our journey, after a hint or two from Donald concerning the length of the way to the next stage, as there was no good halting place between Dalmally and Oban.

Having bid adieu to our venerable and kind cicerone, we proceeded on our tour, winding round the tremendous mountain called Cruachan Ben, which rushes down in all

* This venerable and hospitable gentleman's name was MacIntyre.

its majesty of rocks and wilderness on the lake, leaving only a pass, in which, notwithstanding its extreme strength, the warlike clan of MacDougal of Lorn were almost destroyed by the sagacious Robert Bruce. That King, the Wellington of his day, had accomplished, by a forced march, the unexpected manoeuvre of forcing a body of troops round the other side of the mountain, and thus placed them in the flank and in the rear of the men of Lorn, whom at the same time he attacked in front. The great number of cairns yet visible, as you descend the pass on the westward side, shows the extent of the vengeance which Bruce exhausted on his inveterate and personal enemies. I am, you know, the sister of soldiers, and it has since struck me forcibly that the manoeuvre which Donald described, resembled those of Wellington or of Bonaparte. He was a great man, Robert Bruce, even a Baliol must admit that, although it begins now to be allowed that his title to the crown was scarce so good as that of the unfortunate family with whom he contended – but let that pass. The slaughter had been the greater, as the deep and rapid river Awe is disgorged from the lake, just in the rear of the fugitives, and encircles the base of the tremendous mountain, so that the retreat of the unfortunate fliers was intercepted on all sides by the inaccessible character of the country, which had seemed to promise them defence and protection.

Musing, like the Irish lady in the song, 'upon things which are long enough a-gone',* we felt no impatience at the slow and almost creeping pace with which our conductor proceeded along General Wade's military road, which never or rarely condescends to turn aside from the steepest ascent, but proceeds right up and down hill, with the indifference

* This is a line from a very pathetic ballad which I heard sung by one of the young ladies of Edgeworthstown in 1825. I do not know that it has been printed.

8

to height and hollow, steep or level, indicated by the old Roman engineers. Still, however, the substantial excellence of these great works – for such are the military highways in the Highlands – deserved the compliment of the poet, who, whether he came from our sister kingdom, and spoke in his own dialect, or whether he supposed those whom he addressed might have some national pretension to the second sight, produced the celebrated couplet –

Had you but seen these roads before *they were made,*
You would hold up your hands, and bless General Wade.

Nothing indeed can be more wonderful than to see these wildernesses penetrated and pervious in every quarter by broad accesses of the best possible construction, and so superior to what the country could have demanded for many centuries for any pacific purpose of commercial intercourse. Thus the traces of war are sometimes happily accommodated to the purposes of peace. The victories of Bonaparte have been without results, but his road over the Simplon will long be the communication betwixt peaceful countries, who will apply to the ends of commerce and friendly intercourse that gigantic work which was formed for the ambitious purpose of warlike invasion.

While we were thus stealing along, we gradually turned round the shoulder of Ben Cruachan, and descending the course of the foaming and rapid Awe, left behind us the expanse of the majestic lake which gives birth to that impetuous river. The rocks and precipices which stooped down perpendicularly on our path on the right hand exhibited a few remains of the wood which once clothed them, but which had, in latter times, been felled to supply, Donald MacLeish informed us, the iron-founderies at the Bunawe. This made us fix our eyes with interest on one large oak, which grew on the left hand towards the river. It seemed a tree of extraordinary magnitude and picturesque beauty, and stood just where there appeared to be a few roods of open ground lying among huge stones, which had rolled down from the mountain. To add to the romance of the situation, the spot of clear ground extended round the foot of a proud-browed rock, from the summit of which leaped a mountain stream in a fall of sixty feet, in which it was dissolved into foam and dew. At the bottom of the fall the rivulet with difficulty collected, like a routed general, its dispersed forces, and, as if tamed by its descent, found a noiseless passage through the heath to join the Awe.

I was much struck with the tree and waterfall, and wished myself nearer them; not that I thought of sketchbook or portfolio – for, in my younger days, Misses were not accustomed to black-lead pencils, unless they could use them to some good purpose – but merely to indulge myself with a closer view. Donald immediately opened the chaise door, but observed it was rough walking down the brae, and that I would see the tree better by keeping the road for a hundred yards farther, when it passed closer to the spot, for which he seemed, however, to have no predilection. 'He knew,' he said, 'a far bigger tree than that nearer Bunawe, and it was a place where there was flat ground for the carriage to stand, which it could jimply do on these braes – but just as my leddyship liked.'

My ladyship did choose rather to look at the fine tree before me, than to pass it by in hopes of a finer, so we walked beside the carriage till we should come to a point from which, Donald assured us, we might, without scrambling, go as near the tree as we chose, 'though he wadna advise us to go nearer than the highroad.'

There was something grave and mysterious in Donald's sun-browned countenance when he gave us this intimation, and his manner was so different from his usual frankness, that my female curiosity was set in motion. We walked on the whilst, and I found the tree, of which we had now lost sight by the intervention of some rising ground, was really more distant than I had at first supposed. 'I could have sworn now,' said I to my cicerone, 'that yon tree and waterfall was the very place where you intended to make a stop today.'

'The Lord forbid!' said Donald, hastily.

'And for what, Donald? Why should you be willing to pass so pleasant a spot?'

'It's ower near Dalmally, my leddy, to corn the beasts – it would bring their dinner ower near their breakfast, poor things – an', besides, the place is not canny.'

'Oh! then the mystery is out. There is a bogle or a brownie, a witch or a gyrecarlin, a bodach or a fairy, in the case?'

'The ne'er a bit, my leddy – ye are clean aff the road, as I may say. But if your leddyship will just hae patience, and wait till we are by the place and out of the glen, I'll tell ye all about it. There is no much luck in speaking of such things in the place they chanced in.'

I was obliged to suspend my curiosity, observing that if I persisted in twisting the discourse one way while Donald was twining it another, I should make his objection, like a hempen cord, just so much the tougher. At length the promised turn of the road brought us within fifty paces of the tree which I desired to admire, and I now saw to my surprise that there was a human habitation among the cliffs which surrounded it. It was a hut of the least dimensions, and most miserable description, that I ever saw even in the Highlands. The walls of sod, or *divot*, as the Scotch call it, were not four feet high – the roof was of turf, repaired with reeds and sedges – the chimney was composed of clay, bound round by straw ropes – and the whole walls, roof and chimney were alike covered with the vegetation of house-leek, rye-grass, and moss, common to decayed cottages formed of such materials. There was not the slightest vestige of a kale-yard, the usual accompaniment of the very worst huts, and of living things we saw nothing, save a kid which was browsing on the roof of the hut, and a goat, its mother, at some distance, feeding betwixt the oak and the river Awe.

'What man,' I could not help exclaiming, 'can have committed sin deep enough to deserve such a miserable dwelling!'

'Sin enough,' said Donald MacLeish, with a half-suppressed groan, 'and God he knoweth, misery enough too – and it is no man's dwelling neither, but a woman's.'

'A woman's!' I repeated, 'and in so lonely a place. What sort of a woman can she be?'

'Come this way, my leddy, and you may judge that for yourself,' said Donald. And by advancing a few steps, and making a sharp turn to the left, we gained a sight of the side of the great broad-breasted oak, in the direction opposed to that in which we had hitherto seen it.

'If she keeps her old wont, she will be there at this hour of the day,' said Donald, but immediately became silent, and pointed with his finger, as one afraid of being overheard. I looked, and beheld, not without some sense of awe, a female form seated by the stem of the oak, with her head drooping, her hands clasped, and a dark-coloured mantle drawn over her head, exactly as Judah is represented in the Syrian medals as seated under her palm tree. I was infected with the fear and reverence which my guide seemed to entertain towards this solitary being, nor did I think of advancing towards her to obtain a nearer view until I had cast an enquiring look on Donald, to which he replied in a half whisper, 'She has been a fearfu' bad woman, my leddy.'

'Mad woman, said you?' replied I, hearing him imperfectly, 'then she is perhaps dangerous?'

'No – she is not mad,' replied Donald, 'for then it may be she would be happier than she is, though when she thinks on what she has done, and caused to be done, rather than yield up a hair-breadth of her ain wicked will, it is not likely she can be very well settled. But she neither is mad nor mischievous, and yet, my leddy, I think you had best not go nearer to her.' And then, in a few hurried words, he made me acquainted with the story which I am now to tell more in detail. I heard the narrative with a mixture of horror and sympathy, which at once impelled me to approach the sufferer, and speak to her the words of comfort, or rather of pity, and at the same time made me afraid to do so.

This indeed was the feeling with which she was regarded by the Highlanders in the neighbourhood, who looked upon Elspat MacTavish, or the Woman of the Tree, as they called her, as the Greeks considered those who were pursued by the Furies, and endured the mental torment consequent on great criminal actions. They regarded such unhappy beings as Orestes and Oedipus, as being less the voluntary perpetrators of their crimes than as the passive instruments by which the terrible decrees of Destiny had been accomplished and the fear with which they beheld them was not unmingled with veneration.

I also learned farther from Donald MacLeish that there was some apprehension of ill luck attending those who had the boldness to approach too near, or disturb the awful solitude of a being so unutterably miserable; that it was supposed that whosoever approached her must experience in some respect the contagion of her wretchedness.

It was therefore with some reluctance that Donald saw me prepare to obtain a nearer view of the sufferer, and that he himself followed to assist me in the descent down a very rough path. I believe his regard for me conquered some ominous feelings in his own breast, which connected his duty on this occasion with the presaging fear of lame horses, lost linchpins, overturns, and other perilous chances of the postilion's life.

I am not sure if my own courage would have carried me so close to Elspat, had he not followed. There was in her countenance the stern abstraction of hopeless and over-powering sorrow, mixed with the contending feelings of remorse, and of the pride which struggled to conceal it. She guessed, perhaps, that it was curiosity, arising out of her uncommon story, which induced me to intrude on her solitude – and she could not be pleased that a fate like hers had been the theme of a traveller's amusement. Yet the look with which she regarded me was one of scorn instead of embarrassment. The opinion of the world and all its children could not add or take an iota from her load of misery, and, save from the half smile that seemed to intimate the contempt of a being rapt by the very intensity of her affliction above the sphere of ordinary humanities, she seemed as indifferent to my gaze, as if she had been a dead corpse or a marble statue.

Elspat was above the middle stature. Her hair, now grizzled, was still profuse, and it had been of the most decided black. So were her eyes, in which, contradicting the stern and rigid features of her countenance, there shone the wild and troubled light that indicates an unsettled mind. Her hair was wrapped round a silver bodkin with some attention to neatness, and her dark mantle was disposed around her with a degree of taste, though the materials were of the most ordinary sort.

After gazing on this victim of guilt and calamity till I was ashamed to remain silent, though uncertain how I ought to address her, I began to express my surprise at her choosing such a desert and deplorable dwelling. She cut short these expressions of sympathy, by answering in a stern voice, without the least change of countenance or posture, 'Daughter of the stranger, he has told you my story.' I was silenced at once, and felt how little all earthly accommodation must seem to the mind which had such subjects as hers for rumination. Without again attempting to open the conversation, I took a piece of gold from my purse (for Donald had intimated she lived on alms), expecting she would at least stretch her hand to receive it. But she neither accepted nor rejected the gift – she did not even seem to notice it, though twenty times as valuable, probably, as was usually offered. I was obliged to place it on her knee, saying involuntarily, as I did so, 'May God pardon you, and relieve you!' I shall never forget the look which she cast up to Heaven, nor the tone in which she exclaimed, in the very words of my old friend, John Home –

My beautiful – my brave!

It was the language of nature, and arose from the heart of the deprived mother, as it did from that gifted imaginative poet, while furnishing with appropriate expressions the ideal grief of Lady Randolph.

CHAPTER II

Oh, I'm come to the Low Country,
  Och, och, ohonochie,
Without a penny in my pouch
  To buy a meal for me.
I was the proudest of my clan,
  Long, long may I repine;
And Donald was the bravest man,
  And Donald he was mine.

– Old Song

Elspat had enjoyed happy days, though her age had sunk into hopeless and inconsolable sorrow and distress. She was once the beautiful and happy wife of Hamish MacTavish, for whom his strength and feats of prowess had gained the title of MacTavish Mhor. His life was turbulent and dangerous, his habits being of the old Highland stamp, which esteemed it shame to want any thing that could be had for the taking. Those in the Lowland line who lay near him, and desired to enjoy their lives and property in quiet, were contented to pay him a small composition, in name of protection money, and comforted themselves with the old proverb, that it was better to 'fleech the deil than fight him'. Others, who accounted such composition dishonourable, were often surprised by MacTavish Mhor, and his associates and followers, who usually inflicted an adequate penalty, either in person or property, or both. The creagh is yet remembered in which he swept one hundred and fifty cows from Monteith in one drove, and how he placed the laird of Ballybught naked in a slough for having threatened to send for a party of the Highland Watch to protect his property.

Whatever were occasionally the triumphs of this daring cateran, they were often exchanged for reverses, and his narrow escapes, rapid flights, and the ingenious stratagems with which he extricated himself from imminent danger, were no less remembered and admired than the exploits in which he had been successful. In weal or woe, through every species of fatigue, difficulty and danger, Elspat was his faithful companion. She enjoyed with him the fits of occasional prosperity, and when adversity pressed them hard, her strength of mind, readiness of wit and courageous endurance of danger and toil, are said often to have stimulated the exertions of her husband.

Their morality was of the old Highland cast, faithful friends and fierce enemies: the Lowland herds and harvests they accounted their own, whenever they had the means of driving off the one, or of seizing upon the other, nor did the least scruple on the right of property interfere on such occasions. Hamish Mhor argued like the old Cretan warrior:

My sword, my spear, my shaggy shield,
*   They make me lord of all below;*
For he who dreads the lance to wield,
*   Before my shaggy shield must bow.*
His lands, his vineyards, must resign,
And all that cowards have is mine.

But those days of perilous, though frequently successful depredation, began to be abridged, after the failure of the expedition of Prince Charles Edward. MacTavish Mhor had not sat still on that occasion, and he was outlawed, both as a traitor to the state, and as a robber and cateran. Garrisons were now settled in many places where a redcoat had never before been seen, and the Saxon war-drum resounded among the most hidden recesses of the Highland mountains. The fate of MacTavish became every day more inevitable, and it was the more difficult for him to make his exertions for defence or escape, that Elspat, amid his evil days, had increased his family with an infant child, which was a considerable encumbrance upon the necessary rapidity of their motions.

At length the fatal day arrived. In a strong pass on the skirts of Ben Cruachan, the celebrated MacTavish Mhor was surprised by a detachment of the Sidier Roy.* His wife assisted him heroically, charging his piece from time to time, and as they were in possession of a post that was nearly unassailable, he might have perhaps escaped if his ammunition had lasted. But at length his balls were expended, although it was not until he had fired off most of the silver buttons from his waistcoat, and the soldiers, no longer deterred by fear of the unerring marksman, who had slain three, and wounded more of their number, approached his stronghold, and, unable to take him alive, slew him, after a most desperate resistance.

All this Elspat witnessed and survived, for she had, in the child which relied on her for support, a motive for strength and exertion. In what manner she maintained herself it is not easy to say. Her only ostensible means of support were a flock of three or four goats, which she fed wherever she pleased on the mountain pastures, no one challenging the intrusion. In the general distress of the country, her ancient acquaintances had little to bestow, but what they could part with from their own necessities, they willingly devoted to the relief of others. From Lowlanders she sometimes demanded tribute, rather than requested alms. She had not forgotten she was the widow of MacTavish Mhor, or that the child who trotted by her knee might, such were her imaginations, emulate one day the fame

* The Red Soldier.

of his father, and command the same influence which he had once exerted without control. She associated so little with others, went so seldom and so unwillingly from the wildest recesses of the mountains, where she usually dwelt with her goats, that she was quite unconscious of the great change which had taken place in the country around her, the substitution of civil order for military violence, and the strength gained by the law and its adherents over those who were called in Gaelic song, 'the stormy sons of the sword'. Her own diminished consequence and straitened circumstances she indeed felt, but for this the death of MacTavish Mhor was, in her apprehension, a sufficing reason, and she doubted not that she should rise to her former state of importance, when Hamish Bean (or Fair-haired James) should be able to wield the arms of his father. If, then, Elspat was repelled rudely when she demanded anything necessary for her wants, or the accommodation of her little flock by a churlish farmer, her threats of vengeance, obscurely expressed yet terrible in their tenor, used frequently to extort, through fear of her maledictions, the relief which was denied to her necessities. The trembling goodwife, who gave meal or money to the widow of MacTavish Mhor, wished in her heart that the stern old carlin had been burnt on the day her husband had his due.

Years thus ran on, and Hamish Bean grew up, not indeed to be of his father's size or strength, but to become an active, high-spirited, fair-haired youth, with a ruddy cheek, an eye like an eagle, and all the agility, if not all the strength, of his formidable father, upon whose history and achievements his mother dwelt, in order to form her son's mind to a similar course of adventures. But the young see the present state of this changeful world more keenly than the old. Much attached to his mother, and disposed to do all in his power for her support, Hamish yet perceived, when he mixed with the world, that the trade of the cateran was now alike dangerous and discreditable, and that if he were to emulate his father's prowess, it must be in some other line of warfare more consonant to the opinions of the present day.

As the faculties of mind and body began to expand, he became more sensible of the precarious nature of his situation, of the erroneous views of his mother and her ignorance respecting the changes of the society with which she mingled so little. In visiting friends and neighbours, he became aware of the extremely reduced scale to which his parent was limited, and learned that she possessed little or nothing more than the absolute necessaries of life, and that these were sometimes on the point of failing. At times his success in fishing and the chase was able to add something to her subsistence, but he saw no regular means of contributing to her support, unless by stooping to servile labour, which, if he himself could have endured it, would, he knew, have been like a death's wound to the pride of his mother.

Elspat, meanwhile, saw with surprise that Hamish Bean, although now tall and fit for the field, showed no disposition to enter on his father's scene of action. There was something of the mother at her heart which prevented her from urging him in plain terms to take the field as a cateran, for the fear occurred of the perils into which the trade must conduct him, and when she would have spoken to him on the subject, it seemed to her heated imagination as if the ghost of her husband arose between them in his bloody tartans, and laying his finger on his lips, appeared to prohibit the topic. Yet she wondered at what seemed his want of spirit, sighed as she saw him from day to day lounging about in the long-skirted Lowland coat, which the legislature had imposed upon the

Gael instead of their own romantic garb, and thought how much nearer he would have resembled her husband, had he been clad in the belted plaid and short hose, with his polished arms gleaming at his side.

Besides these subjects for anxiety, Elspat had others arising from the engrossing impetuosity of her temper. Her love of MacTavish Mhor had been qualified by respect and sometimes even by fear, for the cateran was not the species of man who submits to female government, but over his son she had exerted, at first during childhood, and afterwards in early youth, an imperious authority which gave her maternal love a character of jealousy. She could not bear when Hamish, with advancing life, made repeated steps towards independence, absented himself from her cottage at such season and for such length of time as he chose, and seemed to consider, although maintaining towards her every possible degree of respect and kindness, that the control and responsibility of his actions rested on himself alone. This would have been of little consequence, could she have concealed her feelings within her own bosom, but the ardour and impatience of her passions made her frequently show her son that she conceived herself neglected and ill used. When he was absent for any length of time from her cottage, without giving intimation of his purpose, her resentment on his return used to be so unreasonable that it naturally suggested to a young man fond of independence and desirous to amend his situation in the world to leave her, even for the very purpose of enabling him to provide for the parent whose egotistical demands on his filial attention tended to confine him to a desert, in which both were starving in hopeless and helpless indigence.

Upon one occasion, the son having been guilty of some independent excursion by which the mother felt herself affronted and disobliged, she had been more than usually violent on his return, and awakened in Hamish a sense of displeasure which clouded his brow and cheek. At length, as she persevered in her unreasonable resentment, his patience became exhausted, and taking his gun from the chimney corner, and muttering to himself the reply which his respect for his mother prevented him from speaking aloud, he was about to leave the hut which he had but barely entered.

'Hamish,' said his mother, 'are you again about to leave me?' But Hamish only replied by looking at, and rubbing the lock of his gun.

'Ay, rub the lock of your gun,' said his parent, bitterly, 'I am glad you have courage enough to fire it, though it be but at a roe-deer.' Hamish started at this undeserved taunt, and cast a look of anger at her in reply. She saw that she had found the means of giving him pain.

'Yes,' she said, 'look fierce as you will at an old woman, and your mother; it would be long ere you bent your brow on the angry countenance of a bearded man.'

'Be silent, mother, or speak of what you understand,' said Hamish, much irritated, 'and that is of the distaff and the spindle.'

'And was it of spindle and distaff that I was thinking when I bore you away on my back through the fire of six of the Saxon soldiers, and you a wailing child? I tell you, Hamish, I know a hundredfold more of swords and guns than ever you will, and you will never learn so much of noble war by yourself as you have seen when you were wrapped up in my plaid.'

'You are determined at least to allow me no peace at home, mother, but this shall have an end,' said Hamish, as, resuming his purpose of leaving the hut, he rose and went towards the door.

'Stay, I command you,' said his mother, 'stay! or may the gun you carry be the means of your ruin – may the road you are going be the track of your funeral!'

'What makes you use such words, mother?' said the young man, turning a little back. 'They are not good, and good cannot come of them. Farewell just now, we are too angry to speak together – farewell. It will be long ere you see me again.' And he departed, his mother, in the first burst of her impatience, showering after him her maledictions, and in the next invoking them on her own head, so that they might spare her son's. She passed that day and the next in all the vehemence of impotent and yet unrestrained passion, now entreating Heaven, and such powers as were familiar to her by rude tradition, to restore her dear son, 'the calf of her heart', now in impatient resentment, meditating with what bitter terms she should rebuke his filial disobedience upon his return, and now studying the most tender language to attach him to the cottage, which, when her boy was present, she would not, in the rapture of her affection, have exchanged for the apartments of Taymouth Castle.

Two days passed, during which, neglecting even the slender means of supporting nature which her situation afforded, nothing but the strength of a frame accustomed to hardships and privations of every kind could have kept her in existence, notwithstanding the anguish of her mind prevented her being sensible of her personal weakness. Her dwelling, at this period, was the same cottage near which I had found her but then more habitable by the exertions of Hamish, by whom it had been in a great measure built and repaired.

It was on the third day after her son had disappeared, as she sat at the door rocking herself, after the fashion of her countrywomen when in distress or in pain, that the then unwonted circumstance occurred of a passenger being seen on the highroad above the cottage. She cast but one glance at him – he was on horseback, so that it could not be Hamish, and Elspat cared not enough for any other being on earth, to make her turn her eyes towards him a second time. The stranger, however, paused opposite to her cottage, and dismounting from his pony, led it down the steep and broken path which conducted to her door.

'God bless you, Elspat MacTavish!' She looked at the man as he addressed her in her native language with the displeased air of one whose reverie is interrupted, but the traveller went on to say, 'I bring you tidings of your son Hamish.' At once, from being the most uninteresting object, in respect to Elspat, that could exist, the form of the stranger became awful in her eyes, as that of a messenger descended from Heaven, expressly to pronounce upon her death or life. She started from her seat, and with hands convulsively clasped together, and held up to Heaven, eyes fixed on the stranger's countenance, and person stooping forward to him, she looked those enquiries, which her faltering tongue could not articulate. 'Your son sends you his dutiful remembrance and this,' said the messenger, putting into Elspat's hand a small purse containing four or five dollars.

'He is gone, he is gone!' exclaimed Elspat, 'he has sold himself to be the servant of the Saxons, and I shall never more behold him! Tell me, Miles MacPhadraick, for now I know you, is it the price of the son's blood that you have put into the mother's hand?'

'Now, God forbid!' answered MacPhadraick, who was a tacksman, and had possession of a considerable tract of ground under his Chief, a proprietor who lived about twenty miles off – 'God forbid I should do wrong, or say wrong, to you, or to the son of MacTavish Mhor! I swear to you by the hand of my Chief, that your son is well, and will soon see you, and the rest he will tell you himself.' So saying, MacPhadraick hastened back up the pathway, gained the road, mounted his pony, and rode upon his way.

CHAPTER III

Elspat MacTavish remained gazing on the money, as if the impress of the coin could have conveyed information how it was procured.

'I love not this MacPhadraick,' she said to herself, 'it was his race of whom the Bard hath spoken, saying, Fear them not when their words are loud as the winter's wind, but fear them when they fall on you like the sound of the thrush's song. And yet this riddle can be read but one way: my son hath taken the sword, to win that with strength like a man, which churls would keep him from with the words that frighten children.' This idea, when once it occurred to her, seemed the more reasonable, that MacPhadraick, as she well knew, himself a cautious man, had so far encouraged her husband's practices as occasionally to buy cattle of MacTavish, although he must have well known how they were come by, taking care, however, that the transaction was so made as to be accompanied with great profit and absolute safety. Who so likely as MacPhadraick to indicate to a young cateran the glen in which he could commence his perilous trade with most prospect of success? Who so likely to convert his booty into money? The feelings which another might have experienced on believing that an only son had rushed forward on the same path in which his father had perished were scarce known to the Highland mothers of that day. She thought of the death of MacTavish Mhor as that of a hero who had fallen in his proper trade of war, and who had not fallen unavenged. She feared less for her son's life than for his dishonour. She dreaded on his account the subjection to strangers and the death-sleep of the soul which is brought on by what she regarded as slavery.

The moral principle which so naturally and so justly occurs to the mind of those who have been educated under a settled government of laws that protect the property of the weak against the incursions of the strong, was to poor Elspat a book sealed and a fountain closed. She had been taught to consider those whom they call Saxons as a race with whom the Gael were constantly at war, and she regarded every settlement of theirs within the reach of Highland incursion as affording a legitimate object of attack and plunder. Her feelings on this point had been strengthened and confirmed, not only by the desire of revenge for the death of her husband, but by the sense of general indignation entertained, not unjustly, through the Highlands of Scotland, on account of the barbarous and violent conduct of the victors after the battle of Culloden. Other Highland clans, too, she regarded as the fair objects of plunder when that was possible, upon the score of ancient enmities and deadly feuds.

The prudence that might have weighed the slender means which the times afforded for resisting the efforts of a combined government, which had, in its less compact and established authority, been unable to put down the ravages of such lawless caterans as MacTavish Mhor, was unknown to a solitary woman whose ideas still dwelt upon her own early times. She imagined that her son had only to proclaim himself his father's successor in adventure and enterprise, and that a force of men as gallant as those who had followed his father's banner would crowd around to support it when again displayed. To her, Hamish was the eagle who had only to soar aloft and resume his native place in the skies, without her being able to comprehend how many additional eyes would have watched his flight, how many additional bullets would have been directed at his bosom. To be brief, Elspat was one who viewed the present state of society with the same feelings with which she regarded the times that had passed away. She had been indigent, neglected, oppressed, since the days that her husband had no longer been feared and powerful, and she thought that the term of her ascendence would return when her son had determined to play the part of his father. If she permitted her eye to glance farther into futurity, it was but to anticipate that she must be for many a day cold in the grave, with the coronach of her tribe cried duly over her, before her fair-haired Hamish could, according to her calculation, die with his hand on the basket-hilt of the red claymore. His father's hair was grey, ere, after a hundred dangers, he had fallen with his arms in his hands. That she should have seen and survived the sight was a natural consequence of the manners of that age. And better it was – such was her proud thought – that she had seen him so die, than to have witnessed his departure from life in a smoky hovel – on a bed of rotten straw, like an over-worn hound, or a bullock which died of disease. But the hour of her young, her brave Hamish, was yet far distant. He must succeed – he must conquer, like his father. And when he fell at length – for she anticipated for him no bloodless death – Elspat would ere then have lain long in the grave, and could neither see his death struggle, nor mourn over his grave sod.

With such wild notions working in her brain, the spirit of Elspat rose to its usual pitch, or rather to one which seemed higher. In the emphatic language of Scripture, which in that idiom does not greatly differ from her own, she arose, she washed and changed her apparel, and ate bread, and was refreshed.

She longed eagerly for the return of her son, but she now longed not with the bitter anxiety of doubt and apprehension. She said to herself, that much must be done ere he could in these times arise to be an eminent and dreaded leader. Yet when she saw him again, she almost expected him at the head of a daring band, with pipes playing, and banners flying, the noble tartans fluttering free in the wind, in despite of the laws which had suppressed, under severe penalties, the use of the national garb, and all the appurtenances of Highland chivalry. For all this, her eager imagination was content only to allow the interval of some days.

From the moment this opinion had taken deep and serious possession of her mind, her thoughts were bent upon receiving her son at the head of his adherents, in the manner in which she used to adorn her hut for the return of his father.

The substantial means of subsistence she had not the power of providing, nor did she consider that of importance. The successful caterans would bring with them herds and flocks. But the interior of her hut was arranged for their reception – the usquebaugh was brewed or distilled in a larger quantity than it could have been supposed one lone woman could have made ready. Her hut was put into such order as might, in some degree, give it the appearance of a day of rejoicing. It was swept and decorated with boughs of various kinds, like the house of a Jewess, upon what is termed the Feast of the Tabernacles. The produce of the milk of her little flock was prepared in as great variety of forms as her skill admitted, to entertain her son and his associates whom she expected to receive along with him.

But the principal decoration, which she sought with the greatest toil, was the cloud-berry, a scarlet fruit, which is only found on very high hills, and there only in small quantities. Her husband, or perhaps one of his forefathers, had chosen this as the emblem of his family, because it seemed at once to imply by its scarcity the smallness of their clan, and by the places in which it was found, the ambitious height of their pretensions.

For the time that these simple preparations of welcome endured, Elspat was in a state of troubled happiness. In fact, her only anxiety was that she might be able to complete all that she could do to welcome Hamish and the friends whom she supposed must have attached themselves to his band, before they should arrive, and find her unprovided for their reception.

But when such efforts as she could make had been accomplished, she once more had nothing left to engage her save the trifling care of her goats, and when these had been attended to, she had only to review her little preparations, renew such as were of a transitory nature, replace decayed branches and fading boughs, and then to sit down at her cottage door and watch the road, as it ascended on the one side from the banks of the Awe, and on the other wound round the heights of the mountain, with such a degree of accommodation to hill and level as the plan of the military engineer permitted. While so occupied, her imagination, anticipating the future from recollections of the past, formed out of the morning mist or the evening cloud the wild forms of an advancing band, which were then called 'Sidier Dhu' – dark soldiers – dressed in their native tartan, and so named to distinguish them from the scarlet ranks of the British army. In this occupation she spent many hours of each morning and evening.

CHAPTER IV

It was in vain that Elspat's eyes surveyed the distant path, by the earliest light of the dawn and the latest glimmer of the twilight. No rising dust awakened the expectation of nodding plumes or flashing arms – the solitary traveller trudged listlessly along in his brown lowland greatcoat, his tartans dyed black or purple, to comply with or evade the law which prohibited their being worn in their variegated hues. The spirit of the Gael, sunk and broken by the severe though perhaps necessary laws, that proscribed the dress and arms which he considered as his birthright, was intimated by his drooping head and dejected appearance. Not in such depressed wanderers did Elspat recognise the light and free step of her son, now, as she concluded, regenerated from every sign of Saxon thraldom. Night by night, as darkness came, she removed from her unclosed door to throw herself on her restless pallet, not to sleep, but to watch. The brave and the terrible, she said, walk by night – their steps are heard in darkness, when all is silent save the whirlwind and the cataract – the timid deer comes only forth when the sun is upon the mountain's peak, but the bold wolf walks in the red light of the harvest-moon. She reasoned in vain – her son's expected summons did not call her from the lowly couch, where she lay dreaming of his approach. Hamish came not.

'Hope deferred,' saith the royal sage, 'maketh the heart sick,' and strong as was Elspat's constitution, she began to experience that it was unequal to the toils to which her anxious and immoderate affection subjected her, when early one morning the appearance of a traveller on the lonely mountain road, revived hopes which had begun to sink into listless despair. There was no sign of Saxon subjugation about the stranger.

At a distance she could see the flutter of the belted plaid that drooped in graceful folds behind him, and the plume that, placed in the bonnet, showed rank and gentle birth. He carried a gun over his shoulder, the claymore was swinging by his side, with its usual appendages, the dirk, the pistol, and the *sporran mollach*.* Ere yet her eye had scanned all these particulars, the light step of the traveller was hastened, his arm was waved in token of recognition – a moment more, and Elspat held in her arms her darling son, dressed in the garb of his ancestors, and looking, in her maternal eyes, the fairest among ten thousand!

The first outpouring of affection it would be impossible to describe. Blessings mingled with the most endearing epithets which her energetic language affords, in striving to express the wild rapture of Elspat's joy. Her board was heaped hastily with all she had to offer; and the mother watched the young soldier, as he partook of the refreshment, with feelings how similar to, yet how different from, those with which she had seen him draw his first sustenance from her bosom!

When the tumult of joy was appeased, Elspat became anxious to know her son's adventures since they parted, and could not help greatly censuring his rashness for traversing the hills in the Highland dress in the broad sunshine, when the penalty was so heavy, and so many red soldiers were abroad in the country.

'Fear not for me, mother,' said Hamish, in a tone designed to relieve her anxiety, and yet somewhat embarrassed, 'I may wear the *breacan*† at the gate of Fort Augustus, if I like it.'

'Oh, be not too daring, my beloved Hamish, though it be the fault which best becomes thy father's son – yet be not too

* The goatskin pouch, worn by the Highlanders round their waist.
† That which is variegated, i.e. the tartan.

34

daring! Alas, they fight not now as in former days, with fair weapons, and on equal terms, but take odds of numbers and of arms, so that the feeble and the strong are alike levelled by the shot of a boy. And do not think me unworthy to be called your father's widow, and your mother, because I speak thus, for God knoweth, that, man to man, I would peril thee against the best in Breadalbane, and broad Lorn besides.'

'I assure you, my dearest mother,' replied Hamish, 'that I am in no danger. But have you seen MacPhadraick, mother, and what has he said to you on my account?'

'Silver he left me in plenty, Hamish; but the best of his comfort was, that you were well, and would see me soon. But beware of MacPhadraick, my son, for when he called himself the friend of your father, he better loved the most worthless stirk in his herd, than he did the lifeblood of MacTavish Mhor. Use his services, therefore, and pay him for them – for it is thus we should deal with the unworthy – but take my counsel, and trust him not.'

Hamish could not suppress a sigh, which seemed to Elspat to intimate that the caution came too late. 'What have you done with him?' she continued, eager and alarmed. 'I had money of him, and he gives not that without value – he is none of those who exchange barley for chaff. Oh, if you repent you of your bargain, and if it be one which you may break off without disgrace to your truth or your manhood, take back his silver, and trust not to his fair words.'

'It may not be, mother,' said Hamish, 'I do not repent my engagement, unless that it must make me leave you soon.'

'Leave me! how leave me? Silly boy, think you I know not what duty belongs to the wife or mother of a daring man? Thou art but a boy yet, and when thy father had been the dread of the country for twenty years, he did not despise my company and assistance, but often said my help was worth that of two strong gillies.'

'It is not on that score, mother, but since I must leave the country –'

'Leave the country!' replied his mother, interrupting him, 'and think you that I am like a bush, that is rooted to the soil where it grows, and must die if carried elsewhere? I have breathed other winds than these of Ben Cruachan – I have followed your father to the wilds of Ross, and the impenetrable deserts of Y Mac Y Mhor – tush, man, my limbs, old as they are, will bear me as far as your young feet can trace the way.'

'Alas, mother,' said the young man, with a faltering accent, 'but to cross the sea –'

'The sea! who am I that I should fear the sea? Have I never been in a birling in my life – never known the Sound of Mull, the Isles of Treshornish, and the rough rocks of Harris?'

'Alas, mother, I go far, far from all of these – I am enlisted in one of the new regiments, and we go against the French in America.'

'Enlisted!' uttered the astonished mother, 'against *my* will – without *my* consent. You could not – you would not,' – then rising up, and assuming a posture of almost imperial command, 'Hamish, you *dared* not!'

'Despair, mother, dares every thing,' answered Hamish, in a tone of melancholy resolution. 'What should I do here, where I can scarce get bread for myself and you, and when the times are growing daily worse? Would you but sit down and listen, I would convince you I have acted for the best.'

With a bitter smile Elspat sat down, and the same severe ironical expression was on her features, as, with her lips firmly closed, she listened to his vindication.

Hamish went on, without being disconcerted by her expected displeasure. 'When I left you, dearest mother, it was to go to MacPhadraick's house, for although I knew he is crafty and worldly, after the fashion of the Sassenach, yet he is wise, and I thought how he would teach me, as it would cost him nothing, in which way I could mend our estate in the world.'

'Our estate in the world!' said Elspat, losing patience at the word, 'and went you to a base fellow with a soul no better than that of a cowherd, to ask counsel about your conduct? Your father asked none, save of his courage and his sword.'

'Dearest mother,' answered Hamish, 'how shall I convince you that you live in this land of our fathers, as if our fathers were yet living? You walk as it were in a dream, surrounded by the phantoms of those who have been long with the dead. When my father lived and fought, the great respected the man of the strong right hand, and the rich feared him. He had protection from MacAllan Mhor, and from Caberfae,* and tribute from meaner men. That is ended, and his son would only earn a disgraceful and unpitied death, by the practices which gave his father credit and power among those who wear the breacan. The land is conquered – its lights are quenched – Glengary, Lochiel, Perth, Lord Lewis, all the high chiefs are dead or in exile. We may mourn for it, but we cannot help it. Bonnet, broadsword, and sporran – power, strength, and wealth, were all lost on Drummossie Muir.'

'It is false!' said Elspat, fiercely, 'you, and such like dastardly spirits, are quelled by your own faint hearts, not by the strength of the enemy. You are like the fearful waterfowl, to whom the least cloud in the sky seems the shadow of the eagle.'

* Caberfae – *Anglicè*, the Stag's-head, the Celtic designation for the arms of the family of the High Chief of Seaforth.

37

'Mother,' said Hamish, proudly, 'lay not faint heart to my charge. I go where men are wanted who have strong arms and bold hearts too. I leave a desert, for a land where I may gather fame.'

'And you leave your mother to perish in want, age, and solitude,' said Elspat, essaying successively every means of moving a resolution, which she began to see was more deeply rooted than she had at first thought.

'Not so, neither,' he answered, 'I leave you to comfort and certainty, which you have yet never known. Barcaldine's son is made a leader, and with him I have enrolled myself; MacPhadraick acts for him, and raises men, and finds his own in doing it.'

'That is the truest word of the tale, were all the rest as false as hell,' said the old woman, bitterly.

'But we are to find our good in it also,' continued Hamish, 'for Barcaldine is to give you a shieling in his wood of Letter-findreight, with grass for your goats, and a cow, when you please to have one, on the common, and my own pay, dearest mother, though I am far away, will do more than provide you with meal, and with all else you can want. Do not fear for me. I enter a private gentleman, but I will return, if hard fighting and regular duty can deserve it, an officer, and with half a dollar a day.'

'Poor child!' replied Elspat, in a tone of pity mingled with contempt, 'and you trust MacPhadraick?'

'I might, mother,' said Hamish, the dark red colour of his race crossing his forehead and cheeks, 'for MacPhadraick knows the blood which flows in my veins, and is aware, that should he break trust with you, he might count the days which could bring Hamish back to Breadalbane, and number those of his life within three suns more. I would kill him at his own hearth, did he break his word with me – I would, by the great Being who made us both!'

The look and attitude of the young soldier for a moment overawed Elspat. She was unused to see him express a deep and bitter mood, which reminded her so strongly of his father, but she resumed her remonstrances in the same taunting manner in which she had commenced them.

'Poor boy!' she said, 'and you think that at the distance of half the world your threats will be heard or thought of! But, go – go – place your neck under him of Hanover's yoke, against whom every true Gael fought to the death. Go, disown the royal Stewart, for whom your father, and his fathers, and your mother's fathers, have crimsoned many a field with their blood. Go, put your head under the belt of one of the race of Dermid, whose children murdered – yes,' she added, with a wild shriek, 'murdered your mother's fathers in their peaceful dwellings in Glencoe! Yes,' she again exclaimed, with a wilder and shriller scream, 'I was then unborn, but my mother has told me – and I attended to the voice of *my* mother – well I remember her words! They came in peace, and were received in friendship, and blood and fire arose, and screams, and murder!'

'Mother,' answered Hamish, mournfully, but with a decided tone, 'all that I have thought over – there is not a drop of the blood of Glencoe on the noble hand of Barcaldine – with the unhappy house of Glenlyon the curse remains, and on them God hath avenged it.'

'You speak like the Saxon priest already,' replied his mother, 'will you not better stay, and ask a kirk from MacAllan Mhor, that you may preach forgiveness to the race of Dermid?'

'Yesterday was yesterday,' answered Hamish, 'and today is today. When the clans are crushed and confounded together, it is well and wise that their hatreds and their feuds should not survive their independence and their power. He that cannot execute vengeance like a man, should not harbour useless enmity like a craven. Mother, young Barcaldine is true and brave. I know that MacPhadraick counselled him, that he should not let me take leave of you, lest you dissuaded me from my purpose, but he said, "Hamish MacTavish is the son of a brave man, and he will not break his word." Mother, Barcaldine leads an hundred of the bravest of the sons of the Gael in their native dress, and with their fathers' arms – heart to heart – shoulder to shoulder. I have sworn to go with him – He has trusted me, and I will trust him.'

At this reply, so firmly and resolvedly pronounced, Elspat remained like one thunderstruck, and sunk in despair. The arguments which she had considered so irresistibly conclusive, had recoiled like a wave from a rock. After a long pause, she filled her son's quaigh, and presented it to him with an air of dejected deference and submission.

'Drink,' she said, 'to thy father's roof-tree, ere you leave it forever, and tell me – since the chains of a new King, and of a new Chief, whom your fathers knew not save as mortal enemies, are fastened upon the limbs of your father's son – tell me how many links you count upon them?'

Hamish took the cup, but looked at her as if uncertain of her meaning. She proceeded in a raised voice. 'Tell me,' she said, 'for I have a right to know, for how many days the will of those you have made your masters permits me to look upon you? In other words, how many are the days of my life – for when you leave me, the earth has nought besides worth living for!'

'Mother,' replied Hamish MacTavish, 'for six days I may remain with you, and if you will set out with me on the fifth, I will conduct you in safety to your new dwelling. But if you remain here, then I will depart on the seventh by daybreak – then, as at the last moment, I *must* set out for Dunbarton, for if I appear not on the eighth day, I am subject to punishment as a deserter, and am dishonoured as a soldier and a gentleman.'

'Your father's foot,' she answered, 'was free as the wind on the heath – it were as vain to say to him where goest thou, as to ask that viewless driver of the clouds, wherefore blowest thou? Tell me under what penalty thou must – since go thou must, and go thou wilt – return to thy thraldom?'

'Call it not thraldom, mother, it is the service of an honourable soldier – the only service which is now open to the son of MacTavish Mhor.'

'Yet say what is the penalty if thou shouldst not return?' replied Elspat.

'Military punishment as a deserter,' answered Hamish, writhing, however, as his mother failed not to observe, under some internal feelings, which she resolved to probe to the uttermost.

'And that,' she said, with assumed calmness, which her glancing eye disowned, 'is the punishment of a disobedient hound, is it not?'

'Ask me no more, mother,' said Hamish, 'the punishment is nothing to one who will never deserve it.'

'To me it is something,' replied Elspat, 'since I know better than thou, that where there is power to inflict, there is often the will to do so without cause. I would pray for thee, Hamish, and I must know against what evils I should beseech Him who leaves none unguarded, to protect thy youth and simplicity.'

'Mother,' said Hamish, 'it signifies little to what a criminal may be exposed, if a man is determined not to be such. Our Highland chiefs used also to punish their vassals, and, as I have heard, severely. Was it not Lachlan Maclan, whom we

41

remember of old, whose head was struck off by order of his chieftain for shooting at the stag before him?'

'Ay,' said Elspat, 'and right he had to lose it, since he dishonoured the father of the people even in the face of the assembled clan. But the chiefs were noble in their ire – they punished with the sharp blade, and not with the baton. Their punishments drew blood, but they did not infer dishonour. Canst thou say the same for the laws under whose yoke thou hast placed thy freeborn neck?'

'I cannot – mother – I cannot,' said Hamish, mournfully. 'I saw them punish a Sassenach for deserting as they called it, his banner. He was scourged – I own it – scourged like a hound who has offended an imperious master. I was sick at the sight – I confess it. But the punishment of dogs is only for those worse than dogs, who know not how to keep their faith.'

'To this infamy, however, thou hast subjected thyself, Hamish,' replied Elspat, 'if thou shouldst give, or thy officers take, measure of offence against thee. I speak no more to thee on thy purpose. Were the sixth day from this morning's sun my dying day, and thou wert to stay to close mine eyes, thou wouldst run the risk of being lashed like a dog at a post – yes! unless thou hadst the gallant heart to leave me to die alone, and upon my desolate hearth, the last spark of thy father's fire, and of thy forsaken mother's life, to be extinguished together!' Hamish traversed the hut with an impatient and angry pace.

'Mother,' he said at length, 'concern not yourself about such things. I cannot be subjected to such infamy, for never will I deserve it, and were I threatened with it, I should know how to die before I was so far dishonoured.'

'There spoke the son of the husband of my heart!' replied Elspat, and she changed the discourse, and seemed to listen in melancholy acquiescence, when her son reminded her how short the time was which they were permitted to pass in each other's society, and entreated that it might be spent without useless and unpleasant recollections respecting the circumstances under which they must soon be separated.

Elspat was now satisfied that her son, with some of his father's other properties, preserved the haughty masculine spirit which rendered it impossible to divert him from a resolution which he had deliberately adopted. She assumed, therefore, an exterior of apparent submission to their inevitable separation, and if she now and then broke out into complaints and murmurs, it was either that she could not altogether suppress the natural impetuosity of her temper, or because she had the wit to consider, that a total and unreserved acquiescence might have seemed to her son constrained and suspicious, and induced him to watch and defeat the means by which she still hoped to prevent his leaving her. Her ardent, though selfish affection for her son, incapable of being qualified by a regard for the true interests of the unfortunate object of her attachment, resembled the instinctive fondness of the animal race for their offspring, and diving little farther into futurity than one of the inferior creatures, she only felt, that to be separated from Hamish was to die.

In the brief interval permitted them, Elspat exhausted every art which affection could devise, to render agreeable to him the space which they were apparently to spend with each other. Her memory carried her far back into former days, and her stores of legendary history, which furnish at all times a principal amusement of the Highlander in his moments of repose, were augmented by an unusual acquaintance with the songs of ancient bards, and traditions of the most approved Seannachies and tellers of tales. Her officious attentions to her son's accommodation, indeed, were so unremitted as almost to give him pain; and he endeavoured quietly to prevent her from taking so much personal toil in selecting the blooming heath for his bed, or preparing the meal for his refreshment. 'Let me alone, Hamish,' she would reply on such occasions, 'you follow your own will in departing from your mother, let your mother have hers in doing what gives her pleasure while you remain.'

So much she seemed to be reconciled to the arrangements which he had made in her behalf, that she could hear him speak to her of her removing to the lands of Green Colin, as the gentleman was called, on whose estate he had provided her an asylum. In truth, however, nothing could be farther from her thoughts. From what he had said during their first violent dispute, Elspat had gathered, that if Hamish returned not by the appointed time permitted by his furlough, he would incur the hazard of corporal punishment. Were he placed within the risk of being thus dishonoured, she was well aware that he would never submit to the disgrace, by a return to the regiment where it might be inflicted. Whether she looked to any farther probable consequences of her unhappy scheme cannot be known, but the partner of MacTavish Mhor, in all his perils and wanderings, was familiar with an hundred instances of resistance or escape, by which one brave man, amidst a land of rocks, lakes, and mountains, dangerous passes, and dark forests, might baffle the pursuit of hundreds. For the future, therefore, she feared nothing; her sole engrossing object was to prevent her son from keeping his word with his commanding officer.

With this secret purpose, she evaded the proposal which Hamish repeatedly made, that they should set out together to take possession of her new abode, and she resisted it upon grounds apparently so natural to her character, that her son was neither alarmed nor displeased. 'Let me not,' she said, 'in the same short week, bid farewell to my only son, and to the glen in which I have so long dwelt. Let my eye, when dimmed with weeping for thee, still look around, for a while at least, upon Loch Awe and on Ben Cruachan.'

Hamish yielded the more willingly to his mother's humour in this particular, that one or two persons who resided in a neighbouring glen, and had given their sons to Barcaldine's levy, were also to be provided for on the estate of the chieftain, and it was apparently settled that Elspat was to take her journey along with them when they should remove to their new residence. Thus, Hamish believed that he had at once indulged his mother's humour, and ensured her safety and accommodation. But she nourished in her mind very different thoughts and projects!

The period of Hamish's leave of absence was fast approaching, and more than once he proposed to depart, in such time as to ensure his gaining easily and early Dunbarton, the town where were the headquarters of his regiment. But still his mother's entreaties, his own natural disposition to linger among scenes long dear to him, and, above all, his firm reliance in his speed and activity, induced him to protract his departure till the sixth day, being the very last which he could possibly afford to spend with his mother, if indeed he meant to comply with the conditions of his furlough.

CHAPTER V

But for your son, – believe it, oh, believe it –
Most dangerously you have with him prevailed,
If not most mortal to him.–

– Coriolanus

On the evening which preceded his proposed departure, Hamish walked down to the river with his fishing rod, to practise in the Awe, for the last time, a sport in which he excelled, and to find, at the same time, the means for making one social meal with his mother on something better than their ordinary cheer. He was as successful as usual, and soon killed a fine salmon. On his return homeward an incident befell him, which he afterwards related as ominous, though probably his heated imagination, joined to the universal turn of his countrymen for the marvellous, exaggerated into superstitious importance some very ordinary and accidental circumstance.

In the path which he pursued homeward, he was surprised to observe a person, who, like himself, was dressed and armed after the old Highland fashion. The first idea that struck him was, that the passenger belonged to his own corps, who, levied by government, and bearing arms under royal authority, were not amenable for breach of the statutes against the use of the Highland garb or weapons. But he was struck on perceiving, as he mended his pace to make up to his supposed comrade, meaning to request his company for the next day's journey, that the stranger wore a white cockade, the fatal badge which was proscribed in the Highlands. The stature of the man was tall, and there was something shadowy in the outline which added to his size, and his mode of motion, which rather resembled gliding than walking, impressed Hamish with

47

superstitious fears concerning the character of the being which thus passed before him in the twilight. He no longer strove to make up to the stranger, but contented himself with keeping him in view, under the superstition common to the Highlanders, that you ought neither to intrude yourself on such supernatural apparitions as you may witness, nor avoid their presence, but leave it to themselves to withhold or extend their communication, as their power may permit, or the purpose of their commission require.

Upon an elevated knoll by the side of the road, just where the pathway turned down to Elspat's hut, the stranger made a pause and seemed to await Hamish's coming up. Hamish, on his part, seeing it was necessary he should pass the object of his suspicion, mustered up his courage and approached the spot where the stranger had placed himself, who first pointed to Elspat's hut and made, with arm and head, a gesture prohibiting Hamish to approach it, then stretched his hand to the road which led to the southward, with a motion which seemed to enjoin his instant departure in that direction. In a moment afterwards the plaided form was gone – Hamish did not exactly say vanished, because there were rocks and stunted trees enough to have concealed him, but it was his own opinion that he had seen the spirit of MacTavish Mhor, warning him to commence his instant journey to Dunbarton, without waiting till morning, or again visiting his mother's hut.

In fact, so many accidents might arise to delay his journey, especially where there were many ferries, that it became his settled purpose, though he could not depart without bidding his mother adieu, that he neither could nor would abide longer than for that object, and that the first glimpse of next day's sun should see him many miles advanced towards Dunbarton. He descended the path, therefore, and entering the cottage, he communicated, in a hasty and troubled voice, which indicated mental agitation, his determination to take his instant departure. Somewhat to his surprise, Elspat appeared not to combat his purpose, but she urged him to take some refreshment ere he left her for ever. He did so hastily, and in silence, thinking on the approaching separation, and scarce yet believing it would take place without a final struggle with his mother's fondness. To his surprise, she filled the quaigh with liquor for his parting cup.

'Go,' she said, 'my son, since such is thy settled purpose; but first stand once more on thy mother's hearth, the flame on which will be extinguished long ere thy foot shall again be placed there.'

'To your health, mother!' said Hamish, 'and may we meet again in happiness, in spite of your ominous words.'

'It were better not to part,' said his mother, watching him as he quaffed the liquor, of which he would have held it ominous to have left a drop.

'And now,' she said, muttering the words to herself, 'go – if thou canst go.'

'Mother,' said Hamish, as he replaced on the table the empty quaigh, 'thy drink is pleasant to the taste, but it takes away the strength which it ought to give.'

'Such is its first effect, my son,' replied Elspat, 'but lie down upon that soft heather couch, shut your eyes but for a moment, and, in the sleep of an hour, you shall have more refreshment than in the ordinary repose of three whole nights, could they be blended into one.'

'Mother,' said Hamish, upon whose brain the potion was now taking rapid effect, 'give me my bonnet – I must kiss you and begone – yet it seems as if my feet were nailed to the floor.'

'Indeed,' said his mother, 'you will be instantly well, if you will sit down for half an hour – but half an hour: it is eight hours to dawn, and dawn were time enough for your father's son to begin such a journey.'

'I must obey you, mother – I feel I must,' said Hamish, inarticulately, 'but call me when the moon rises.'

He sat down on the bed – reclined back, and almost instantly was fast asleep. With the throbbing glee of one who has brought to an end a difficult and troublesome enterprise, Elspat proceeded tenderly to arrange the plaid of the unconscious slumberer, to whom her extravagant affection was doomed to be so fatal, expressing, while busied in her office, her delight, in tones of mingled tenderness and triumph. 'Yes,' she said, 'calf of my heart, the moon shall arise and set to thee, and so shall the sun, but not to light thee from the land of thy fathers, or tempt thee to serve the foreign prince or the feudal enemy! To no son of Dermid shall I be delivered, to be fed like a bondswoman, but he who is my pleasure and my pride shall be my guard and my protector. They say the Highlands are changed, but I see Ben Cruachan rear his crest as high as ever into the evening sky – no one hath yet herded his kine on the depths of Loch Awe – and yonder oak does not yet bend like a willow. The children of the mountains will be such as their fathers, until the mountains themselves shall be levelled with the strath. In these wild forests, which used to support thousands of the brave, there is still surely subsistence and refuge left for one aged woman, and one gallant youth, of the ancient race and the ancient manners.'

While the misjudging mother thus exulted in the success of her stratagem, we may mention to the reader, that it was founded on the acquaintance with drugs and simples, which Elspat, accomplished in all things belonging to the wild life which she had led, possessed in an uncommon degree, and which she exercised for various purposes. With the herbs, which she knew how to select as well as how to distil, she could relieve more diseases than a regular medical person could easily believe. She applied some to dye the bright colours of the tartan – from others she compounded draughts of various powers, and unhappily possessed the secret of one which was strongly soporific. Upon the effects of this last concoction, as the reader doubtless has anticipated, she reckoned with security on delaying Hamish beyond the period for which his return was appointed, and she trusted to his horror for the apprehended punishment to which he was thus rendered liable, to prevent him from returning at all.

Sound and deep, beyond natural rest, was the sleep of Hamish MacTavish on that eventful evening, but not such the repose of his mother. Scarce did she close her eyes from time to time, but she awakened again with a start, in the terror that her son had arisen and departed, and it was only on approaching his couch, and hearing his deep-drawn and regular breathing, that she reassured herself of the security of the repose in which he was plunged.

Still, dawning, she feared, might awaken him, notwithstanding the unusual strength of the potion with which she had drugged his cup. If there remained a hope of mortal man accomplishing the journey, she was aware that Hamish would attempt it, though he were to die from fatigue upon the road. Animated by this new fear, she studied to exclude the light, by stopping all the crannies and crevices through which, rather than through any regular entrance, the morning beams might find access to her miserable dwelling, and this in order to detain amid its wants and wretchedness the being, on whom, if the world itself had been at her disposal, she would have joyfully conferred it.

Her pains were bestowed unnecessarily. The sun rose high above the heavens, and not the fleetest stag in Breadalbane, were the hounds at his heels, could have sped, to save his life, so fast as would have been necessary to keep Hamish's appointment. Her purpose was fully attained – her son's return within the period assigned was impossible. She deemed it equally impossible, that he would ever dream of returning, standing, as he must now do, in the danger of an infamous punishment. By degrees, and at different times, she had gained from him a full acquaintance with the predicament in which he would be placed by failing to appear on the day appointed, and the very small hope he could entertain of being treated with lenity. It is well known that the great and wise Earl of Chatham prided himself on the scheme, by which he drew together for the defence of the colonies, those hardy Highlanders, who, until his time, had been the objects of doubt, fear, and suspicion, on the part of each successive administration. But some obstacles occurred, from the peculiar habits and temper of this people, to the execution of his patriotic project. By nature and habit, every Highlander was accustomed to the use of arms, but at the same time totally unaccustomed to, and impatient of, the restraints imposed by discipline upon regular troops. They were a species of militia, who had no conception of a camp as their only home. If a battle was lost, they dispersed to save themselves, and look out for the safety of their families; if won, they went back to their glens to hoard up their booty, and attend to their cattle and their farms. This privilege of going and coming at pleasure they would not be deprived of even by their Chiefs, whose authority was in most other respects so despotic. It followed as a matter of course that the new-levied Highland recruits could scarce be made to comprehend the nature of a military engagement, which compelled a man to serve in the army longer than he pleased, and perhaps, in many instances, sufficient care was not taken at enlisting to explain to them the permanency of the engagement which they came under, lest such a disclosure should induce them to change their mind. Desertions were therefore become numerous from the newly-raised regiment, and the veteran General who commanded at Dunbarton, saw no better way of checking them than by causing an unusually severe example to be made of a deserter from an English corps. The young Highland regiment was obliged to attend upon the punishment, which struck a people peculiarly jealous of personal honour with equal horror and disgust, and not unnaturally indisposed some of them to the service. The old General, however, who had been regularly bred in the German wars, stuck to his own opinion, and gave out in orders that the first Highlander, who might either desert or fail to appear at the expiry of his furlough, should be brought to the halberds and punished like the culprit whom they had seen in that condition. No man doubted that General — would keep his word rigorously whenever severity was required, and Elspat, therefore, knew that her son, when he perceived that due compliance with his orders was impossible, must at the same time consider the degrading punishment denounced against his defection as inevitable, should he place himself within the General's power.

When noon was well passed, new apprehensions came on the mind of the lonely woman. Her son still slept under the influence of the draught, but what if, being stronger than she had ever known it administered, his health or his reason should be affected by its potency? For the first time, likewise, notwithstanding her high ideas on the subject of parental authority, she began to dread the resentment of her son, whom her heart told her she had wronged. Of late, she had observed that his temper was less docile, and his determinations, especially upon this late occasion of his enlistment, independently formed, and then boldly carried through. She remembered the stern wilfulness of his father when he accounted himself ill-used, and began to dread that Hamish, upon finding the deceit she had put upon him, might resent it even to the extent of cutting her off, and pursuing his own course through the world alone. Such were the alarming and yet the reasonable apprehensions which began to crowd upon the unfortunate woman, after the apparent success of her ill-advised stratagem.

It was near evening when Hamish first awoke, and then he was far from being in the full possession either of his mental or bodily powers. From his vague expressions and disordered pulse, Elspat at first experienced much apprehension, but she used such expedients as her medical knowledge suggested, and in the course of the night, she had the satisfaction to see him sink once more into a deep sleep, which probably carried off the greater part of the effects of the drug, for about sunrising she heard him arise, and call to her for his bonnet. This she had purposely removed, from a fear that he might awaken and depart in the night-time, without her knowledge.

'My bonnet – my bonnet,' cried Hamish, 'it is time to take farewell. Mother, your drink was too strong – the sun is up – but with the next morning I will still see the double summit of the ancient Dun. My bonnet – my bonnet! mother, I must be instant in my departure.' These expressions made it plain that poor Hamish was unconscious that two nights and a day had passed since he had drained the fatal quaigh, and Elspat had now to venture on what she felt as the almost perilous, as well as painful task, of explaining her machinations.

'Forgive me, my son,' she said, approaching Hamish, and taking him by the hand with an air of deferential awe, which perhaps she had not always used to his father, even when in his moody fits.

'Forgive you, mother – for what?' said Hamish, laughing, 'for giving me a dram that was too strong, and which my head still feels this morning, or for hiding my bonnet to keep me an instant longer? Nay, do *you* forgive *me*. Give me the bonnet, and let that be done which now must be done. Give me my bonnet, or I go without it; surely I am not to be delayed by so trifling a want as that – I, who have gone for years with only a strap of deer's hide to tie back my hair. Trifle not, but give it me, or I must go bareheaded, since to stay is impossible.'

'My son,' said Elspat, keeping fast hold of his hand, 'what is done cannot be recalled. Could you borrow the wings of yonder eagle, you would arrive at the Dun too late for what you purpose – too soon for what awaits you there. You believe you see the sun rising for the first time since you have seen him set, but yesterday beheld him climb Ben Cruachan, though your eyes were closed to his light.'

Hamish cast upon his mother a wild glance of extreme terror, then instantly recovering himself, said, 'I am no child to be cheated out of my purpose by such tricks as these – Farewell, mother, each moment is worth a lifetime.'

'Stay,' she said, 'my dear – my deceived son! run not on infamy and ruin. Yonder I see the priest upon the high road on his white horse – ask him the day of the month and week – let him decide between us.'

With the speed of an eagle, Hamish darted up the acclivity, and stood by the minister of Glenorquhy, who was pacing out thus early to administer consolation to a distressed family near Bunawe.

The good man was somewhat startled to behold an armed Highlander, then so unusual a sight, and apparently much agitated, stop his horse by the bridle, and ask him with a faltering voice the day of the week and month. 'Had you been where you should have been yesterday, young man,' replied the clergyman, 'you would have known that it was God's Sabbath, and that this is Monday, the second day of the week, and twenty-first of the month.'

'And this is true?' said Hamish.

'As true,' answered the surprised minister, 'as that I yesterday preached the word of God to this parish. What ails you, young man? – are you sick? – are you in your right mind?'

Hamish made no answer, only repeated to himself the first expression of the clergyman, 'Had you been where you should have been yesterday,' and so saying, he let go the bridle, turned from the road, and descended the path towards the hut, with the look and pace of one who was going to execution. The minister looked after him with surprise, but although he knew the inhabitant of the hovel, the character of Elspat had not invited him to open any communication with her, because she was generally reputed a Papist, or rather one indifferent to all religion, except some superstitious observances which had been handed down from her parents. On Hamish the Reverend Mr Tyrie had bestowed instructions when he was occasionally thrown in his way, and if the seed fell among the brambles and thorns of a wild and uncultivated disposition, it had not yet been entirely checked or destroyed. There was something so ghastly in the present expression of the youth's features, that the good man was tempted to go down to the hovel, and enquire whether any distress had befallen the inhabitants, in which his presence might be consoling, and his ministry useful. Unhappily he did not persevere in this resolution, which might have saved a great misfortune, as he would have probably become a mediator for the unfortunate young man; but a recollection of the wild moods of such Highlanders as had been educated after the old fashion of the country, prevented his interesting himself in the widow and son of the far-dreaded robber MacTavish Mhor; and he thus missed an opportunity, which he afterwards sorely repented, of doing much good.

When Hamish MacTavish entered his mother's hut, it was only to throw himself on the bed he had left, and, exclaiming, 'Undone, undone!' to give vent, in cries of grief and anger, to his deep sense of the deceit which had been practised on him, and of the cruel predicament to which he was reduced.

Elspat was prepared for the first explosion of her son's passion, and said to herself, 'It is but the mountain torrent, swelled by the thunder shower. Let us sit and rest us by the bank; for all its present tumult, the time will soon come when we may pass it dryshod.' She suffered his complaints and his reproaches, which were, even in the midst of his agony, respectful and affectionate, to die away without returning any answer; and when, at length, having exhausted all the exclamations of sorrow which his language, copious in expressing the feelings of the heart, affords to the sufferer, he sunk into a gloomy silence, she suffered the interval to continue near an hour ere she approached her son's couch.

'And now,' she said at length, with a voice in which the authority of the mother was qualified by her tenderness, 'have you exhausted your idle sorrows, and are you able to place what you have gained against what you have lost? Is the false son of Dermid your brother, or the father of your tribe, that you weep because you cannot bind yourself to his belt, and become one of those who must do his bidding? Could you find in yonder distant country the lakes and the mountains that you leave behind you here? Can you hunt the deer of Breadalbane in the forests of America, or will the ocean afford you the silver-scaled salmon of the Awe? Consider, then, what is your loss, and, like a wise man, set it against what you have won.'

'I have lost all, mother,' replied Hamish, 'since I have broken my word, and lost my honour. I might tell my tale, but who, oh, who would believe me?' The unfortunate young man again clasped his hands together, and, pressing them to his forehead, hid his face upon the bed.

Elspat was now really alarmed, and perhaps wished the fatal deceit had been left unattempted. She had no hope or refuge saving in the eloquence of persuasion, of which she possessed no small share, though her total ignorance of the world as it actually existed, rendered its energy unavailing. She urged her son, by every tender epithet which a parent could bestow, to take care for his own safety.

'Leave me,' she said, 'to baffle your pursuers. I will save your life – I will save your honour – I will tell them that my fair-haired Hamish fell from the Corrie dhu* into the gulf, of which human eye never beheld the bottom. I will tell them this, and I will fling your plaid on the thorns which grow on the brink of the precipice, that they may believe my words. They will believe, and they will return to the Dun of the double-crest, for though the Saxon drum can call the living to die, it cannot recall the dead to their slavish standard. Then will we travel together far northward to the salt lakes of Kintail, and place glens and mountains betwixt us and the sons of Dermid. We will visit the shores of the dark lake, and my kinsmen – for was not my mother of the children of Kenneth, and will they not

* Black precipice.

58

remember us with the affection of the olden time, which lives in those distant glens, where the Gael still dwell in their nobleness, unmingled with the churl Saxons, or with the base brood that are their tools and their slaves.'

The energy of the language, somewhat allied to hyperbole, even in its most ordinary expressions, now seemed almost too weak to afford Elspat the means of bringing out the splendid picture which she presented to her son of the land in which she proposed to him to take refuge. Yet the colours were few with which she could paint her Highland paradise. 'The hills,' she said, 'were higher and more magnificent than those of Breadalbane – Ben Cruachan was but a dwarf to Skooroora. The lakes were broader and larger, and abounded not only with fish, but with the enchanted and amphibious animal which gives oil to the lamp.* The deer were larger and more numerous – the white-tusked boar, the chase of which the brave loved best, was yet to be roused in those western solitudes – the men were nobler, wiser, and stronger than the degenerate brood who lived under the Saxon banner. The daughters of the land were beautiful, with blue eyes and fair hair, and bosoms of snow, and out of these she would choose a wife for Hamish, of blameless descent, spotless fame, fixed and true affection, who should be in their summer bothy as a beam of the sun, and in their winter abode as the warmth of the needful fire.'

Such were the topics with which Elspat strove to soothe the despair of her son, and to determine him, if possible, to leave the fatal spot, on which he seemed resolved to linger. The style of her rhetoric was poetical, but in other respects resembled that which, like other fond mothers, she had lavished on Hamish while a child or a boy, in order to gain his consent

* The seals are considered by the Highlanders as enchanted princes.

to do something he had no mind t,; and she spoke louder, quicker, and more earnestly, in proportion as she began to despair of her words carrying conviction.

On the mind of Hamish her eloquence made no impression. He knew far better than she did the actual situation of the country, and was sensible that, though it might be possible to hide himself as a fugitive among more distant mountains, there was now no corner in the Highlands in which his father's profession could be practised, even if he had not adopted, from the improved ideas of the time when he lived, the opinion that the trade of the cateran was no longer the road to honour and distinction. Her words were therefore poured into regardless ears, and she exhausted herself in vain in the attempt to paint the regions of her mother's kinsmen in such terms as might tempt Hamish to accompany her thither. She spoke for hours, but she spoke in vain. She could extort no answer, save groans and sighs, and ejaculations, expressing the extremity of despair.

At length, starting on her feet, and changing the monotonous tone in which she had chanted, as it were, the praises of the province of refuge, into the short, stern language of eager passion, 'I am a fool,' she said, 'to spend my words upon an idle, poor-spirited, unintelligent boy, who crouches like a hound to the lash. Wait here, and receive your taskmasters, and abide your chastisement at their hands; but do not think your mother's eyes will behold it. I could not see it and live. My eyes have looked often upon death, but never upon dishonour. Farewell, Hamish! We never meet again.'

She dashed from the hut like a lapwing, and perhaps for the moment actually entertained the purpose which she expressed, of parting with her son for ever. A fearful sight she would have been that evening to any who might have met her wandering through the wilderness like a restless spirit, and speaking to herself in language which will endure no translation. She rambled for hours, seeking rather than shunning the most dangerous paths. The precarious track through the morass, the dizzy path along the edge of the precipice, or by the banks of the gulfing river, were the roads which, far from avoiding, she sought with eagerness, and traversed with reckless haste. But the courage arising from despair was the means of saving the life, which (though deliberate suicide was rarely practised in the Highlands) she was perhaps desirous of terminating. Her step on the verge of the precipice was firm as that of the wild goat. Her eye, in that state of excitation, was so keen as to discern, even amid darkness, the perils which noon would not have enabled a stranger to avoid.

Elspat's course was not directly forward, else she had soon been far from the bothy in which she had left her son. It was circuitous, for that hut was the centre to which her heart-strings were chained, and though she wandered around it, she felt it impossible to leave the vicinity. With the first beams of morning, she returned to the hut. A while she paused at the wattled door, as if ashamed that lingering fondness should have brought her back to the spot which she had left with the purpose of never returning, but there was yet more of fear and anxiety in her hesitation – of anxiety, lest her fair-haired son had suffered from the effects of her potion – of fear, lest his enemies had come upon him in the night. She opened the door of the hut gently, and entered with noiseless step. Exhausted with his sorrow and anxiety, and not entirely relieved perhaps from the influence of the powerful opiate, Hamish Bean again slept the stern sound sleep, by which the Indians are said to be overcome during the interval of their torments. His mother was scarcely sure that she actually discerned his form on the bed, scarce certain that her ear caught the sound of his breathing. With a throbbing heart, Elspat went to the fireplace in the centre of the hut, where slumbered, covered with a piece of turf, the glimmering embers of the fire, never extinguished on a Scottish hearth until the indwellers leave the mansion for ever.

'Feeble greishogh,'* she said, as she lighted, by the help of a match, a splinter of bog pine which was to serve the place of a candle, 'weak greishogh, soon shalt thou be put out for ever, and may Heaven grant that the life of Elspat MacTavish have no longer duration than thine!'

While she spoke she raised the blazing light towards the bed, on which still lay the prostrate limbs of her son, in a posture that left it doubtful whether he slept or swooned. As she advanced towards him, the light flashed upon his eyes – he started up in an instant, made a stride forward with his naked dirk in his hand, like a man armed to meet a mortal enemy, and exclaimed, 'Stand off! – on thy life, stand off!'

'It is the word and the action of my husband,' answered Elspat, 'and I know by his speech and his step the son of MacTavish Mhor.'

'Mother,' said Hamish, relapsing from his tone of desperate firmness into one of melancholy expostulation, 'oh, dearest mother, wherefore have you returned hither?'

'Ask why the hind comes back to the fawn,' said Elspat, 'why the cat of the mountain returns to her lodge and her young. Know you, Hamish, that the heart of the mother only lives in the bosom of the child.'

'Then will it soon cease to throb,' said Hamish, 'unless it can beat within a bosom that lies beneath the turf. Mother, do not blame me; if I weep, it is not for myself but for you,

* Greishogh, a glowing ember.

for my sufferings will soon be over, but yours – O who but Heaven shall set a boundary to them!'

Elspat shuddered and stepped backward, but almost instantly resumed her firm and upright position, and her dauntless bearing.

'I thought thou wert a man but even now,' she said, 'and thou art again a child. Hearken to me yet, and let us leave this place together. Have I done thee wrong or injury? If so, yet do not avenge it so cruelly. See, Elspat MacTavish, who never kneeled before even to a priest, falls prostrate before her own son, and craves his forgiveness.' And at once she threw herself on her knees before the young man, seized on his hand, and kissing it an hundred times, repeated as often, in heartbreaking accents, the most earnest entreaties for forgiveness. 'Pardon,' she exclaimed, 'pardon, for the sake of your father's ashes – pardon, for the sake of the pain with which I bore thee, the care with which I nurtured thee! Hear it, Heaven, and behold it, Earth – the mother asks pardon of her child, and she is refused!'

It was in vain that Hamish endeavoured to stem this tide of passion, by assuring his mother, with the most solemn asseverations, that he forgave entirely the fatal deceit which she had practised upon him.

'Empty words,' she said, 'idle protestations, which are but used to hide the obduracy of your resentment. Would you have me believe you, then leave the hut this instant, and retire from a country which every hour renders more dangerous. Do this, and I may think you have forgiven me – refuse it, and again I call on moon and stars, heaven and earth, to witness the unrelenting resentment with which you prosecute your mother for a fault, which, if it be one, arose out of love to you.'

'Mother,' said Hamish, 'on this subject you move me not. I will fly before no man. If Barcaldine should send every Gael that is under his banner, here, and in this place, will I abide them, and when you bid me fly, you may as well command yonder mountain to be loosened from its foundations. Had I been sure of the road by which they are coming hither, I had spared them the pains of seeking me, but I might go by the mountain, while they perchance came by the lake. Here I will abide my fate, nor is there in Scotland a voice of power enough to bid me stir from hence, and be obeyed.'

'Here, then, I also stay,' said Elspat, rising up and speaking with assumed composure. 'I have seen my husband's death – my eyelids shall not grieve to look on the fall of my son. But MacTavish Mhor died as became the brave, with his good sword in his right hand; my son will perish like the bullock that is driven to the shambles by the Saxon owner, who has bought him for a price.'

'Mother,' said the unhappy young man, 'you have taken my life; to that you have a right, for you gave it, but touch not my honour! It came to me from a brave train of ancestors, and should be sullied neither by man's deed nor woman's speech. What I shall do, perhaps I myself yet know not, but tempt me no farther by reproachful words; you have already made wounds more than you can ever heal.'

'It is well, my son,' said Elspat, in reply. 'Expect neither farther complaint nor remonstrance from me, but let us be silent, and wait the chance which Heaven shall send us.'

The sun arose on the next morning, and found the bothy silent as the grave. The mother and son had arisen, and were engaged each in their separate task – Hamish in preparing and cleaning his arms with the greatest accuracy, but with an air of deep dejection. Elspat, more restless in her agony of spirit, employed herself in making ready the food which the distress of yesterday had induced them both to dispense with for an unusual number of hours. She placed it on the board before her son so soon as it was prepared, with the words of a Gaelic poet: 'Without daily food, the husbandman's ploughshare stands still in the furrow; without daily food, the sword of the warrior is too heavy for his hand. Our bodies are our slaves, yet they must be fed if we would have their service. So spake, in ancient days, the Blind Bard to the warriors of Fion.'

The young man made no reply, but he fed on what was placed before him, as if to gather strength for the scene which he was to undergo. When his mother saw that he had eaten what sufficed him, she again filled the fatal quaigh, and proffered it as the conclusion of the repast. But he started aside with a convulsive gesture, expressive at once of fear and abhorrence.

'Nay, my son,' she said, 'this time surely, thou hast no cause of fear.'

'Urge me not, mother,' answered Hamish, 'or put the leprous toad into a flagon, and I will drink, but from that accursed cup, and of that mind-destroying potion, never will I taste more!'

'At your pleasure, my son,' said Elspat, haughtily, and began, with much apparent assiduity, the various domestic tasks which had been interrupted during the preceding day. Whatever was at her heart, all anxiety seemed banished from her looks and demeanour. It was but from an over activity of bustling exertion that it might have been perceived, by a close observer, that her actions were spurred by some internal cause of painful excitement, and such a spectator, too, might also have observed how often she broke off the snatches of songs or tunes which she hummed, apparently without knowing what she was doing, in order to cast a hasty glance from the door of the hut. Whatever might be in the mind of Hamish, his demeanour was directly the reverse of that adopted by his mother. Having finished the task of cleaning and preparing his arms, which he arranged within the hut, he sat himself down before the door of the bothy, and watched the opposite hill, like the fixed sentinel who expects the approach of an enemy. Noon found him in the same unchanged posture, and it was an hour after that period, when his mother, standing beside him, laid her hand on his shoulder, and said, in a tone indifferent, as if she had been talking of some friendly visit, 'When dost thou expect them?'

'They cannot be here till the shadows fall long to the eastward,' replied Hamish, 'that is, even supposing the nearest party, commanded by Sergeant Allan Breack Cameron, has been commanded hither by express from Dunbarton, as it is most likely they will.'

'Then enter beneath your mother's roof once more, partake the last time of the food which she has prepared. After this, let them come, and thou shalt see if thy mother is an useless encumbrance in the day of strife. Thy hand, practised as it is, cannot fire these arms so fast as I can load them; nay, if it is necessary, I do not myself fear the flash or the report, and my aim has been held fatal.'

'In the name of Heaven, mother, meddle not with this matter!' said Hamish. 'Allan Breack is a wise man and a kind one, and comes of a good stem. It may be, he can promise for our officers, that they will touch me with no infamous punishment, and if they offer me confinement in the dungeon, or death by the musket, to that I may not object.'

'Alas! and wilt thou trust to their word, my foolish child? Remember the race of Dermid were ever fair and false, and no sooner shall they have gyves on thy hands, than they will strip thy shoulders for the scourge.'

'Save your advice, mother,' said Hamish, sternly, 'for me, my mind is made up.'

But though he spoke thus, to escape the almost persecuting urgency of his mother, Hamish would have found it, at that moment, impossible to say upon what course of conduct he had thus fixed. On one point alone he was determined, namely, to abide his destiny, be what it might, and not to add to the breach of his word, of which he had been involuntarily rendered guilty, by attempting to escape from punishment. This act of self-devotion he conceived to be due to his own honour, and that of his countrymen. Which of his comrades would in future be trusted, if he should be considered as having broken his word, and betrayed the confidence of his officers? And whom but Hamish Bean MacTavish would the Gael accuse, for having verified and confirmed the suspicions which the Saxon General was well known to entertain against the good faith of the Highlanders? He was, therefore, bent firmly to abide his fate. But whether his intention was to yield himself peaceably into the hands of the party who should come to apprehend him, or whether he purposed, by a show of resistance, to provoke them to kill him on the spot, was a question which he could not himself have answered. His desire to see Barcaldine, and explain the cause of his absence at the appointed time, urged him to the one course; his fear of the degrading punishment, and of his mother's bitter upbraidings, strongly instigated the latter and the more dangerous purpose. He left it to chance to decide when the crisis should arrive; nor did he tarry long in expectation of the catastrophe.

Evening approached, the gigantic shadows of the mountains streamed in darkness towards the east, while their western peaks were still glowing with crimson and gold. The road which winds round Ben Cruachan was fully visible from the door of the bothy, when a party of five Highland soldiers, whose arms glanced in the sun, wheeled suddenly into sight from the most distant extremity where the highway is hidden behind the mountain. One of the party walked a little before the other four, who marched regularly and in files, according to the rules of military discipline. There was no dispute, from the firelocks which they carried, and the plaids and bonnets which they wore, that they were a party of Hamish's regiment, under a non-commissioned officer, and there could be as little doubt of the purpose of their appearance on the banks of Loch Awe.

'They come briskly forward,' said the widow of MacTavish Mhor, 'I wonder how fast or how slow some of them will return again! But they are five, and it is too much odds for a fair field. Step back within the hut, my son, and shoot from the loophole beside the door. Two you may bring down ere they quit the high road for the footpath – there will remain but three, and your father, with my aid, has often stood against that number.'

Hamish Bean took the gun which his mother offered, but did not stir from the door of the hut. He was soon visible to the party on the high road, as was evident from their increasing their pace to a run, the files, however, still keeping together like coupled greyhounds, and advancing with great rapidity. In far less time than would have been accomplished by men less accustomed to the mountains, they had left the high road, traversed the narrow path, and approached within pistol-shot of the bothy, at the door of which stood Hamish, fixed like a statue of stone, with his firelock in his hand, while his mother, placed behind him, and almost driven to frenzy by the violence of her passions, reproached him in the strongest terms which despair could invent, for his want of resolution and faintness of heart. Her words increased the bitter gall which was arising in the young man's own spirit, as he observed the unfriendly speed with which his late comrades were eagerly making towards him, like hounds towards the stag when he is at bay. The untamed and angry passions which he inherited from father and mother were awakened by the supposed hostility of those who pursued him, and the restraint under which these passions had been hitherto held by his sober judgment began gradually to give way. The sergeant now called to him, 'Hamish Bean MacTavish, lay down your arms and surrender.'

'Do *you* stand, Allan Breack Cameron, and command your men to stand, or it will be the worse for us all.'

'Halt, men!' said the sergeant, but continuing himself to advance. 'Hamish, think what you do, and give up your gun; you may spill blood, but you cannot escape punishment.'

'The scourge – the scourge – my son, beware the scourge!' whispered his mother.

'Take heed, Allan Breack,' said Hamish. 'I would not hurt you willingly – but I will not be taken unless you can assure me against the Saxon lash.'

'Fool!' answered Cameron, 'you know I cannot. Yet I will do all I can. I will say I met you on your return, and the punishment will be light – but give up your musket. Come on, men.'

Instantly he rushed forward, extending his arm as if to push aside the young man's levelled firelock. Elspat exclaimed, 'Now, spare not your father's blood to defend your father's hearth!' Hamish fired his piece, and Cameron dropped dead. All these things happened, it might be said, in the same moment of time. The soldiers rushed forward and seized Hamish, who, seeming petrified with what he had done, offered not the least resistance. Not so his mother, who, seeing the men about to put handcuffs on her son, threw herself on the soldiers with such fury, that it required two of them to hold her, while the rest secured the prisoner.

'Are you not an accursed creature,' said one of the men to Hamish, 'to have slain your best friend, who was contriving, during the whole march, how he could find some way of getting you off without punishment for your desertion?'

'Do you hear *that*, mother?' said Hamish, turning himself as much towards her as his bonds would permit – but the mother heard nothing, and saw nothing. She had fainted on the floor of her hut. Without waiting for her recovery, the party almost immediately began their homeward march towards Dunbarton, leading along with them their prisoner. They thought it necessary, however, to stay for a little space at the village of Dalmally, from which they despatched a party of the inhabitants to bring away the body of their unfortunate leader, while they themselves repaired to a magistrate to state what had happened, and require his instructions as to the farther course to be pursued. The crime being of a military character, they were instructed to march the prisoner to Dunbarton without delay.

The swoon of the mother of Hamish lasted for a length of time, the longer perhaps that her constitution, strong as it was, must have been much exhausted by her previous agitation of three days' endurance. She was roused from her stupor at length by female voices, which cried the coronach, or lament for the dead, with clapping of hands and loud exclamations, while the melancholy note of a lament, appropriate to the clan Cameron, played on the bagpipe, was heard from time to time.

Elspat started up like one awakened from the dead, and without any accurate recollection of the scene which had passed before her eyes. There were females in the hut who were swathing the corpse in its bloody plaid before carrying it from the fatal spot. 'Women,' she said, starting up and interrupting their chant at once and their labour, 'tell me, women, why sing you the dirge of MacDhonuil Dhu in the house of MacTavish Mhor?'

'She-wolf, be silent with thine ill-omened yell,' answered one of the females, a relation of the deceased, 'and let us do our duty to our beloved kinsman! There shall never be coronach cried, or dirge played, for thee or thy bloody wolf-burd.* The ravens shall eat him from the gibbet, and the foxes and wild-cats shall tear thy corpse upon the hill. Cursed be he that would sain your bones, or add a stone to your cairn!'

'Daughter of a foolish mother,' answered the widow of MacTavish Mhor, 'know that the gibbet with which you threaten us is no portion of our inheritance. For thirty years the Black Tree of the Law, whose apples are dead men's bodies, hungered after the beloved husband of my heart, but he died like a brave man, with the sword in his hand, and defrauded it of its hopes and its fruit.'

'So shall it not be with thy child, bloody sorceress,' replied the female mourner, whose passions were as violent as those of Elspat herself. 'The ravens shall tear his fair hair to line their nests, before the sun sinks beneath the Treshornish islands.'

These words recalled to Elspat's mind the whole history of the last three dreadful days. At first she stood fixed as if the extremity of distress had converted her into stone, but in a minute, the pride and violence of her temper, outbraved as she thought herself on her own threshold, enabled her to

* Wolf-brood, i. e. wolf-cub.

reply, 'Yes, insulting hag, my fair-haired boy may die, but it will not be with a white hand – it has been dyed in the blood of his enemy, in the best blood of a Cameron – remember that, and when you lay your dead in his grave, let it be his best epitaph, that he was killed by Hamish Bean for essaying to lay hands on the son of MacTavish Mhor on his own threshold. Farewell – the shame of defeat, loss, and slaughter, remain with the clan that has endured it!'

The relative of the slaughtered Cameron raised her voice in reply, but Elspat, disdaining to continue the objurgation, or perhaps feeling her grief likely to overmaster her power of expressing her resentment, had left the hut, and was walking forth in the bright moonshine.

The females who were arranging the corpse of the slaughtered man hurried from their melancholy labour to look after her tall figure as it glided away among the cliffs. 'I am glad she is gone,' said one of the younger persons who assisted. 'I would as soon dress a corpse when the great Fiend himself – God sain us – stood visibly before us, as when Elspat of the Tree is amongst us. Ay – ay, even overmuch intercourse hath she had with the Enemy in her day.'

'Silly woman,' answered the female who had maintained the dialogue with the departed Elspat, 'thinkest thou that there is a worse fiend on earth, or beneath it, than the pride and fury of an offended woman, like yonder bloody-minded hag? Know that blood has been as familiar to her as the dew to the mountain daisy. Many and many a brave man has she caused to breathe their last for little wrong they had done to her or theirs. But her hough-sinews are cut, now that her wolf-burd must, like a murderer as he is, make a murderer's end.'

Whilst the women thus discoursed together, as they watched the corpse of Allan Breack Cameron, the unhappy cause of his death pursued her lonely way across the mountain. While she remained within sight of the bothy, she put a strong constraint on herself, that by no alteration of pace or gesture, she might afford to her enemies the triumph of calculating the excess of her mental agitation, nay, despair. She stalked, therefore, with a slow rather than a swift step, and, holding herself upright, seemed at once to endure with firmness that woe which was passed, and bid defiance to that which was about to come. But when she was beyond the sight of those who remained in the hut, she could no longer suppress the extremity of her agitation. Drawing her mantle wildly round her, she stopped at the first knoll, and climbing to its summit, extended her arms up to the bright moon, as if accusing heaven and earth for her misfortunes, and uttered scream on scream, like those of an eagle whose nest has been plundered of her brood. Awhile she vented her grief in these inarticulate cries, then rushed on her way with a hasty and unequal step, in the vain hope of overtaking the party which was conveying her son a prisoner to Dunbarton. But her strength, superhuman as it seemed, failed her in the trial, nor was it possible for her, with her utmost efforts, to accomplish her purpose.

Yet she pressed onward, with all the speed which her exhausted frame could exert. When food became indispensable, she entered the first cottage. 'Give me to eat,' she said, 'I am the widow of MacTavish Mhor – I am the mother of Hamish MacTavish Bean – give me to eat, that I may once more see my fair-haired son.' Her demand was never refused, though granted in many cases with a kind of struggle between compassion and aversion in some of those to whom she applied, which was in others qualified by fear. The share she had had in occasioning the death of Allan Breack Cameron, which must probably involve that of her own son, was not accurately known, but, from a knowledge of her violent passions and former habits of life, no one doubted that in one way or other she had been the cause of the catastrophe, and Hamish Bean was considered, in the slaughter which he had committed, rather as the instrument than as the accomplice of his mother.

This general opinion of his countrymen was of little service to the unfortunate Hamish. As his captain, Green Colin, understood the manners and habits of his country, he had no difficulty in collecting from Hamish the particulars accompanying his supposed desertion, and the subsequent death of the non-commissioned officer. He felt the utmost compassion for a youth, who had thus fallen a victim to the extravagant and fatal fondness of a parent. But he had no excuse to plead which could rescue his unhappy recruit from the doom, which military discipline and the award of a court-martial denounced against him for the crime he had committed.

No time had been lost in their proceedings, and as little was interposed betwixt sentence and execution. General — had determined to make a severe example of the first deserter who should fall into his power, and here was one who had defended himself by main force, and slain in the affray the officer sent to take him into custody. A fitter subject for punishment could not have occurred and Hamish was sentenced to immediate execution. All which the interference of his captain in his favour could procure, was that he should die a soldier's death, for there had been a purpose of executing him upon the gibbet.

The worthy clergyman of Glenorquhy chanced to be at Dunbarton, in attendance upon some church courts, at the time of this catastrophe. He visited his unfortunate parishioner in his dungeon, found him ignorant indeed, but not obstinate, and the answers which he received from him, when conversing on religious topics, were such as induced him doubly to regret, that a mind naturally pure and noble should have remained unhappily so wild and uncultivated.

When he ascertained the real character and disposition of the young man, the worthy pastor made deep and painful reflections on his own shyness and timidity, which, arising out of the evil fame that attached to the lineage of Hamish, had restrained him from charitably endeavouring to bring this strayed sheep within the great fold. While the good minister blamed his cowardice in times past, which had deterred him from risking his person, to save, perhaps, an immortal soul, he resolved no longer to be governed by such timid counsels, but to endeavour, by application to his officers, to obtain a reprieve, at least, if not a pardon, for the criminal, in whom he felt so unusually interested, at once from his docility of temper and his generosity of disposition.

Accordingly, the divine sought out Captain Campbell at the barracks within the garrison. There was a gloomy melancholy on the brow of Green Colin, which was not lessened, but increased, when the clergyman stated his name, quality, and errand. 'You cannot tell me better of the young man than I am disposed to believe,' answered the Highland officer, 'you cannot ask me to do more in his behalf than I am of myself inclined, and have already endeavoured to do. But it is all in vain. General — is half a Lowlander, half an Englishman. He has no idea of the high and enthusiastic character which in these mountains often brings exalted virtues in contact with great crimes, which, however, are less offences of the heart than errors of the understanding. I have gone so far as to tell him that, in this young man, he was putting to death the best and the bravest of my company, where all, or almost all, are good and brave. I explained to him by what strange delusion the culprit's apparent desertion was occasioned, and how little his heart was accessory to the crime which his hand unhappily committed. His answer was, "These are Highland visions, Captain Campbell, as unsatisfactory and vain as those of the second sight. An act of gross desertion may, in any case, be palliated under the plea of intoxication; the murder of an officer may be as easily coloured over with that of temporary insanity. The example must be made, and if it has fallen on a man otherwise a good recruit, it will have the greater effect." Such being the General's unalterable purpose,' continued Captain Campbell, with a sigh, 'be it your care, reverend sir, that your penitent prepare, by break of day tomorrow, for that great change which we shall all one day be subjected to.'

'And for which,' said the clergyman, 'may God prepare us all, as I in my duty will not be wanting to this poor youth.'

Next morning, as the very earliest beams of sunrise saluted the grey towers which crown the summit of that singular and tremendous rock, the soldiers of the new Highland regiment appeared on the parade, within the Castle of Dunbarton, and having fallen into order, began to move downward by steep staircases, and narrow passages towards the external barrier-gate, which is at the very bottom of the rock. The wild wailings of the pibroch were heard at times, interchanged with the drums and fifes, which beat the Dead March.

The unhappy criminal's fate did not, at first, excite that general sympathy in the regiment which would probably have arisen had he been executed for desertion alone. The slaughter of the unfortunate Allan Breack had given a different colour to Hamish's offence, for the deceased was much beloved, and besides belonged to a numerous and powerful clan, of whom there were many in the ranks. The unfortunate criminal, on the contrary, was little known to, and scarcely connected with, any of his regimental companions. His father had been, indeed, distinguished for his strength and manhood, but he was of a broken clan, as those names were called who had no chief to lead them to battle.

It would almost have been impossible, in another case, to have turned out of the ranks of the regiment the party necessary for execution of the sentence, but the six individuals selected for that purpose were friends of the deceased, descended, like him, from the race of MacDhonuil Dhu, and while they prepared for the dismal task which their duty imposed, it was not without a stern feeling of gratified revenge. The leading company of the regiment began now to defile from the barrier-gate, and was followed by the others, each successively moving and halting according to the orders of the Adjutant, so as to form three sides of an oblong square, with the ranks faced inwards. The fourth, or blank side of the square, was closed up by the huge and lofty precipice on which the Castle rises. About the centre of the procession, bare-headed, disarmed, and with his hands bound, came the unfortunate victim of military law. He was deadly pale, but his step was firm and his eye as bright as ever. The clergyman walked by his side – the coffin, which was to receive his mortal remains, was borne before him. The looks of his comrades were still, composed, and solemn. They felt for the youth, whose handsome form and manly yet submissive deportment had, as soon as he was distinctly visible to them, softened the hearts of many, even of some who had been actuated by vindictive feelings.

The coffin destined for the yet living body of Hamish Bean was placed at the bottom of the hollow square, about two yards distant from the foot of the precipice, which rises in that place as steep as a stone wall to the height of three or four hundred feet. Thither the prisoner was also led, the clergyman still continuing by his side, pouring forth exhortations of courage and consolation, to which the youth appeared to listen with respectful devotion. With slow, and, it seemed, almost unwilling steps, the firing party entered the square, and were drawn up facing the prisoner, about ten yards distant. The clergyman was now about to retire. 'Think, my son,' he said, 'on what I have told you, and let your hope be rested on the anchor which I have given. You will then exchange a short and miserable existence here, for a life in which you will experience neither sorrow nor pain. Is there aught else which you can entrust to me to execute for you?'

The youth looked at his sleeve buttons. They were of gold, booty perhaps which his father had taken from some English officer during the civil wars. The clergyman disengaged them from his sleeves.

'My mother!' he said with some effort, 'give them to my poor mother! See her, good father, and teach her what she should think of all this. Tell her Hamish Bean is more glad to die than ever he was to rest after the longest day's hunting. Farewell, sir – farewell!'

The good man could scarce retire from the fatal spot. An officer afforded him the support of his arm. At his last look towards Hamish, he beheld him alive and kneeling on the coffin; the few that were around him had all withdrawn. The fatal word was given, the rock rung sharp to the sound of the discharge, and Hamish, falling forward with a groan, died, it may be supposed, without almost a sense of the passing agony.

Ten or twelve of his own company then came forward, and laid with solemn reverence the remains of their comrade in the coffin, while the Dead March was again struck up, and the several companies, marching in single files, passed the coffin one by one, in order that all might receive from the awful spectacle the warning which it was peculiarly intended to afford. The regiment was then marched off the ground, and reascended the ancient cliff, their music, as usual on such occasions, striking lively strains, as if sorrow, or even deep thought, should as short a while as possible be the tenant of the soldier's bosom.

At the same time the small party, which we before mentioned, bore the bier of the ill-fated Hamish to his humble grave, in a corner of the churchyard of Dunbarton, usually assigned to criminals. Here, among the dust of the guilty, lies a youth, whose name, had he survived the ruin of the fatal events by which he was hurried into crime, might have adorned the annals of the brave.

The minister of Glenorquhy left Dunbarton immediately after he had witnessed the last scene of this melancholy catastrophe. His reason acquiesced in the justice of the sentence, which required blood for blood, and he acknowledged that the vindictive character of his countrymen required to be powerfully restrained by the strong curb of social law. But still he mourned over the individual victim. Who may arraign the bolt of Heaven when it bursts among the sons of the forest, yet who can refrain from mourning, when it selects for the object of its blighting aim the fair stem of a young oak, that promised to be the pride of the dell in which it flourished? Musing on these melancholy events, noon found him engaged in the mountain passes, by which he was to return to his still distant home.

Confident in his knowledge of the country, the clergyman had left the main road to seek one of those shorter paths which are only used by pedestrians, or by men, like the minister, mounted on the small but sure-footed, hardy and sagacious horses of the country. The place which he now traversed, was in itself gloomy and desolate, and tradition had added to it the terror of superstition, by affirming it was haunted by an evil spirit, termed *Cloght-dearg*, that is, Redmantle, who at all times, but especially at noon and at midnight, traversed the glen, in enmity both to man and the inferior creation, did such evil as her power was permitted to extend to, and afflicted with ghastly terrors those whom she had not licence otherwise to hurt.

The minister of Glenorquhy had set his face in opposition to many of these superstitions, which he justly thought were derived from the dark ages of Popery, perhaps even from those of Paganism, and unfit to be entertained or believed by the Christians of an enlightened age. Some of his more attached parishioners considered him as too rash in opposing the ancient faith of their fathers, and though they honoured the moral intrepidity of their pastor, they could not avoid entertaining and expressing fears, that he would one day fall a victim to his temerity, and be torn to pieces in the glen of the Cloght-dearg, or some of those other haunted wilds, which he appeared rather to have a pride and pleasure in traversing alone, on the days and hours when the wicked spirits were supposed to have especial power over man and beast.

These legends came across the mind of the clergyman, and, solitary as he was, a melancholy smile shaded his cheek as he thought of the inconsistency of human nature, and reflected how many brave men, whom the yell of the pibroch would have sent headlong against fixed bayonets, as the wild bull rushes on his enemy, might have yet feared to encounter those visionary terrors, which he himself, a man of peace, and in ordinary perils no way remarkable for the firmness of his nerves, was now risking without hesitation.

As he looked around the scene of desolation, he could not but acknowledge, in his own mind, that it was not ill chosen for the haunt of those spirits, which are said to delight in solitude and desolation. The glen was so steep and narrow that there was but just room for the meridian sun to dart a few scattered rays upon the gloomy and precarious stream which stole through its recesses, for the most part in silence, but occasionally murmuring sullenly against the rocks and large stones, which seemed determined to bar its further progress. In winter, or in the rainy season, this small stream was a foaming torrent of the most formidable magnitude, and it was at such periods that it had torn open and laid bare the broad-faced and huge fragments of rock, which, at the season of which we speak, hid its course from the eye, and seemed disposed totally to interrupt its course. 'Undoubtedly,' thought the clergyman, 'this mountain rivulet, suddenly swelled by a waterspout, or thunderstorm, has often been the cause of those accidents, which, happening in the glen called by her name, have been ascribed to the agency of the Cloght-dearg.'

Just as this idea crossed his mind, he heard a female voice exclaim, in a wild and thrilling accent, 'Michael Tyrie – Michael Tyrie!' He looked round in astonishment, and not without some fear. It seemed for an instant as if the Evil Being, whose existence he had disowned, was about to appear for the punishment of his incredulity. This alarm did not hold him more than an instant, nor did it prevent his replying in a firm voice, 'Who calls – and where are you?'

'One who journeys in wretchedness, between life and death,' answered the voice, and the speaker, a tall female, appeared from among the fragments of rocks which had concealed her from view.

As she approached more closely, her mantle of bright tartan, in which the red colour much predominated, her stature, the long stride with which she advanced, and the writhen features and wild eyes which were visible from under her curch, would have made her no inadequate representative of the spirit which gave name to the valley. But Mr Tyrie instantly knew her as the Woman of the Tree, the widow of MacTavish Mhor, the now childless mother of Hamish Bean. I am not sure whether the minister would not have endured the visitation of the Cloght-dearg herself, rather than the shock of Elspat's presence, considering her crime and her misery. He drew up his horse instinctively, and stood endeavouring to collect his ideas, while a few paces brought her up to his horse's head.

'Michael Tyrie,' said she, 'the foolish women of the Clachan* hold thee as a god – be one to me, and say that my son lives. Say this, and I too will be of thy worship – I will bend my knees on the seventh day in thy house of worship, and thy God shall be my God.'

'Unhappy woman,' replied the clergyman, 'man forms not pactions with his Maker as with a creature of clay like himself. Thinkest thou to chaffer with Him, who formed the earth, and spread out the heavens, or that thou canst offer aught of homage or devotion that can be worth acceptance in his eyes? He hath asked obedience, not sacrifice; patience under the trials with which he afflicts us, instead of vain bribes, such as man offers to his changeful brother of clay, that he may be moved from his purpose.'

'Be silent, priest!' answered the desperate woman, 'speak not to me the words of thy white book. Elspat's kindred were

* i.e. The village, literally the stones.

of those who crossed themselves and knelt when the sacring bell was rung, and she knows that atonement can be made on the altar for deeds done in the field. Elspat had once flocks and herds, goats upon the cliffs, and cattle in the strath. She wore gold around her neck and on her hair – thick twists as those worn by the heroes of old. All these would she have resigned to the priest – all these, and if he wished for the ornaments of a gentle lady, or the sporran of a high chief, though they had been great as Macallanmore himself, MacTavish Mhor would have procured them if Elspat had promised them. Elspat is now poor, and has nothing to give. But the Black Abbot of Inchaffray would have bidden her scourge her shoulders, and macerate her feet by pilgrimage, and he would have granted his pardon to her when he saw that her blood had flowed, and that her flesh had been torn. These were the priests who had indeed power even with the most powerful – they threatened the great men of the earth with the word of their mouth, the sentence of their book, the blaze of their torch, the sound of their sacring bell. The mighty bent to their will, and unloosed at the word of the priests those whom they had bound in their wrath, and set at liberty, unharmed, him whom they had sentenced to death, and for whose blood they had thirsted. These were a powerful race, and might well ask the poor to kneel, since their power could humble the proud. But you! – against whom are ye strong, but against women who have been guilty of folly, and men who never wore sword? The priests of old were like the winter torrent which fills this hollow valley, and rolls these massive rocks against each other as easily as the boy plays with the ball which he casts before him. But you! you do but resemble the summer-stricken stream, which is turned aside by the rushes, and stemmed by a bush of sedges. Woe worth you, for there is no help in you!'

The clergyman was at no loss to conceive that Elspat had lost the Roman Catholic faith without gaining any other, and that she still retained a vague and confused idea of the composition with the priesthood, by confession, alms, and penance, and of their extensive power, which, according to her notion, was adequate, if duly propitiated, even to effecting her son's safety. Compassionating her situation, and allowing for her errors and ignorance, he answered her with mildness.

'Alas, unhappy woman! Would to God I could convince thee as easily where thou oughtest to seek, and art sure to find consolation, as I can assure you with a single word, that were Rome and all her priesthood once more in the plenitude of their power, they could not, for largesse or penance, afford to thy misery an atom of aid or comfort. Elspat MacTavish, I grieve to tell you the news.'

'I know them without thy speech,' said the unhappy woman, 'my son is doomed to die.'

'Elspat,' resumed the clergyman, 'he *was* doomed, and the sentence has been executed.'

The hapless mother threw her eyes up to heaven, and uttered a shriek so unlike the voice of a human being, that the eagle which soared in middle air answered it as she would have done the call of her mate.

'It is impossible!' she exclaimed, 'it is impossible! Men do not condemn and kill on the same day! Thou art deceiving me. The people call thee holy – hast thou the heart to tell a mother she has murdered her only child?'

'God knows,' said the priest, the tears falling fast from his eyes, 'that, were it in my power, I would gladly tell better tidings – but these which I bear are as certain as they are fatal. My own ears heard the death-shot, my own eyes beheld thy son's death – thy son's funeral. My tongue bears witness to what my ears heard and my eyes saw.'

The wretched female clasped her hands close together, and held them up towards heaven like a sibyl announcing war and desolation, while, in impotent yet frightful rage, she poured forth a tide of the deepest imprecations. 'Base Saxon churl!' she exclaimed, 'vile hypocritical juggler! May the eyes that looked tamely on the death of my fair-haired boy be melted in their sockets with ceaseless tears, shed for those that are nearest and most dear to thee! May the ears that heard his death-knell be dead hereafter to all other sounds save the screech of the raven, and the hissing of the adder! May the tongue that tells me of his death and of my own crime, be withered in thy mouth – or better, when thou wouldst pray with thy people, may the Evil One guide it, and give voice to blasphemies instead of blessings, until men shall fly in terror from thy presence, and the thunder of heaven be launched against thy head, and stop for ever thy cursing and accursed voice! Begone, with this malison! Elspat will never, never again bestow so many words upon living man.'

She kept her word – from that day the world was to her a wilderness, in which she remained without thought, care, or interest, absorbed in her own grief, indifferent to everything else.

With her mode of life, or rather of existence, the reader is already as far acquainted as I have the power of making him. Of her death, I can tell him nothing. It is supposed to have happened several years after she had attracted the attention of my excellent friend Mrs Bethune Baliol. Her benevolence, which was never satisfied with dropping a sentimental tear, when there was room for the operation of effective charity, induced her to make various attempts to alleviate the condition of this most wretched woman. But all her exertions could only render Elspat's means of subsistence less precarious, a circumstance which, though generally interesting even to the most wretched outcasts seemed to her a matter of total indifference. Every attempt to place any person in her hut to take charge of her miscarried, through the extreme resentment with which she regarded all intrusion on her solitude, or by the timidity of those who had been pitched upon to be inmates with the terrible Woman of the Tree. At length, when Elspat became totally unable (in appearance at least) to turn herself on the wretched settle which served her for a couch, the humanity of Mr Tyrie's successor sent two women to attend upon the last moments of the solitary, which could not, it was judged, be far distant, and to avert the possibility that she might perish for want of assistance or food, before she sunk under the effects of extreme age, or mortal malady.

It was on a November evening that the two women appointed for this melancholy purpose arrived at the miserable cottage which we have already described. Its wretched inmate lay stretched upon the bed, and seemed almost already a lifeless corpse, save for the wandering of the fierce dark eyes, which rolled in their sockets in a manner terrible to look upon, and seemed to watch with surprise and indignation the motions of the strangers, as persons whose presence was alike unexpected and unwelcome. They were frightened at her looks; but, assured in each other's company, they kindled a fire, lighted a candle, prepared food, and made other arrangements for the discharge of the duty assigned them.

The assistants agreed they should watch the bedside of the sick person by turns, but, about midnight, overcome by fatigue (for they had walked far that morning) both of them fell fast asleep. When they awoke, which was not till after the interval of some hours, the hut was empty, and the patient gone. They rose in terror, and went to the door of the cottage, which was latched as it had been at night. They looked out into the darkness, and called upon their charge by her name. The night-raven screamed from the old oak tree, the fox howled on the hill, the hoarse waterfall replied with its echoes, but there was no human answer. The terrified women did not dare to make further search till morning should appear, for the sudden disappearance of a creature so frail as Elspat, together with the wild tenor of her history, intimidated them from stirring from the hut. They remained, therefore, in dreadful terror, sometimes thinking they heard her voice without, and at other times, that sounds of a different description were mingled with the mournful sigh of the night breeze, or the dash of the cascade. Sometimes, too, the latch rattled, as if some frail and impotent hand were in vain attempting to lift it, and ever and anon they expected the entrance of their terrible patient animated by supernatural strength, and in the company, perhaps, of some being more dreadful than herself. Morning came at length. They sought brake, rock, and thicket, in vain. Two hours after daylight, the minister himself appeared, and, on the report of the watchers, caused the country to be alarmed, and a general and exact search to be made through the whole neighbourhood of the cottage and the oak tree. But it was all in vain. Elspat MacTavish was never found, whether dead or alive, nor could there ever be traced the slightest circumstance to indicate her fate.

The neighbourhood was divided concerning the cause of her disappearance. The credulous thought that the Evil Spirit, under whose influence she seemed to have acted, had carried her away in the body, and there are many who are still unwilling, at untimely hours, to pass the oak tree, beneath which, as they allege, she may still be seen seated according to her wont. Others less superstitious supposed, that had it been possible to search the gulf of the Corrie Dhu, the profound deeps of the lake, or the whelming eddies of the river, the remains of Elspat MacTavish might have been discovered, as nothing was more natural, considering her state of body and mind, than that she should have fallen in by accident, or precipitated herself intentionally into one or other of those places of sure destruction. The clergyman entertained an opinion of his own. He thought that, impatient of the watch which was placed over her, this unhappy woman's instinct had taught her, as it directs various domestic animals, to withdraw herself from the sight of her own race, that the death struggle might take place in some secret den, where, in all probability, her mortal relics would never meet the eyes of mortals. This species of instinctive feeling seemed to him of a tenor with the whole course of her unhappy life, and most likely to influence her, when it drew to a conclusion.

Sir Walter Scott was born in College Wynd, Edinburgh, on 15th August 1771, the ninth child of Walter Scott, Writer to the Signet, and Anne Rutherford, though not all of the children survived. At the age of two he contracted polio, which left him lame in the right leg. In an attempt to cure both the polio and its after-effects, he was sent to stay with his grandfather in the Scottish Borders, and thus began a lifelong interest in these regions. Much of his early youth was spent in travelling to seek alleviation of the symptoms of his polio.

In 1779, he began attending the High School of Edinburgh, and in 1783, aged twelve, he enrolled at the University of Edinburgh, where he studied Classics, although his health again failed while he was in attendance at the University. In 1786, aged fifteen, he began a solicitors' apprenticeship at his father's firm, culminating in his being called to the Bar in 1792. Around the time of beginning his apprenticeship, he made his first trip to the Scottish Highlands, and also began to attend literary salons, meeting Robert Burns at the age of just fifteen. In 1789 he returned to university to read law, qualifying in 1792 and practising in Edinburgh.

In 1797, after a thwarted love affair with Williamina Belsches had left him heartbroken, he met Charlotte Charpentier of Lyons in France, whom he married in 1797. They lived together in Edinburgh until 1804, during which time they had two daughters and a son, and Scott was appointed Sheriff-Deputy of Selkirkshire. It was also at this time that he began to publish literary works, initially translations of works by German Romantic authors, and then in 1802–3 the three-volume set of Scottish ballads *The Minstrelsy of the Scottish Border*. He continued to publish poetry, and among his most famous works are *Marmion* (1808) and *The Lady of the Lake* (1810).

In 1804 Scott and his wife moved to Galashiels in the Scottish Borders, and in 1805 had a second son. During this period, Scott became involved in publishing, entering into the industry first with his friend James Ballantyne, and then with his brother John, whose publishing company John Ballantyne & Co. he came to half own. In 1809 Scott co-founded the *Quarterly Review*, and in 1812 the family moved to Abbotsford House, a home built by Scott. In 1813, however, John Ballantyne & Co. collapsed and was bought out by Constable & Co., who became Scott's publishers. At this time, perhaps for reasons of financial expediency, he turned his attention from poetry to fiction, and published *Waverley* anonymously in 1814. Following the enormous success of this work, he went on to write a series of novels including *Rob Roy* (1817) and *Ivanhoe* (1819), all under the pen name 'The Author of Waverley'.

In 1820 he accepted a baronetcy, and in 1822 played a principal role in arranging the visit of King George IV to Scotland, an event which helped to establish tartan and kilts as items of Scottish national identity. In 1825, however, his fortunes again began to collapse as his publishing company again hit bankruptcy. Writing prolifically in order to stave off financial ruin, in the final years of his life he produced works including *Chronicles of the Canongate* (1827) and, in the same year, a biography of Napoleon Bonaparte. It was also at this time that he officially avowed authorship of the many novels written under the name 'The Author of Waverley'. He died at his home, Abbotsford House, on 21st September 1832.